A RAINY AFFAIR

ANTHONY PATHFINDER

Published by EastSouth Publishing LLC
www.eastsouthpublishing.com

For more information, or to contact the author:

www.anthonypathfinder.com
authoranthonypathfinder@gmail.com

The cataloging-in-publication data is on file with the Library of Congress.

ISBN 9780615825939 (paperback)
ISBN 9798812033569 (hardcover)

This book was printed in the United States of America

This book is dedicated to the women who dared to walk away from their abusive relationships.

I want to thank my children who mean the world to me. I love you. I would like to recognize several of my fellow authors: Brooklen Borne, Beverly "Dimples" Rowley, Savannah J, Dena Tyson, and Laurie Bowler.

EPISODE
1

She wandered around the city dazed and confused. Her mind was playing tricks on her. Everything seemed out of place as her thirst and hunger overtook any rational thoughts she had. As the fast-moving throng of New Yorkers made their way through the crowded Times Square streets, Rain Banks-Summer, a thirty-something-year-old, wondered what would become of her. Visions of her past flashed in front of her eyes as she thought about the chain of events that took her from her childhood home to the city where dreams are made.

A natural chocolate brown beauty, smart, intelligent, and outgoing, she stood five-eleven with shoulder-length dark hair. Blessed with an amazingly sexy physique, she was quite the looker, easy on the eyes so to speak.

Nonetheless, this wasn't the case as she walked unsteadily with dry parched lips trying to make sense of how her life had suddenly changed.

She had been traveling for some time without food or water. It was only when the Greyhound bus she was traveling on stopped at one of the many eateries along the highway that she was able to quench her thirst. She waited until no one was looking before asking the person behind the counter for a drink of water. If it were too crowded, she would drink from the sink in the lady's room.

The hunger was making her delusional. Her vision was blurred. Any sense of direction that she had was now a thing of the past as she bumped into several angry New Yorkers trying to make their way home.

***

It wasn't that long ago she bolted her Bloomfield Hills, Michigan home from an abusive husband. To make matters worse, he wanted an open relationship — something she wanted no part of. The mental, emotional, and physical abuse was too much. After months of considering it, she decided to leave.

She had to endure the name-calling and disrespect, that she had become used to. He was arrogant, mean-spirited, and self-centered. He shared their bedroom with other women as well.

Rain begged and pleaded with him to stop, but he would have none of it. When she asked for a divorce, he refused. He was in charge of the finances and saw to it that she never had more than what he thought she needed. He refused to get her pregnant, and when she would complain that she wanted children, he would respond by saying, "An architect does not make a whole lot of money, and don't you see the life of luxury we live? Don't you see where we live? Why would you want to change that by adding more expenses? Besides, I like my women in shape, not out of shape, so forget about it," he would say mockingly, knowing quite well they led a successful life.

She had made a terrible mistake by falling in love with Jonathan Banks. He convinced her to disown her family and move in with him in his Bloomfield Hills home. Originally from Toledo, Florida, Rain was from a prominent family and led a fairly decent life. A college graduate and aspiring writer, she somehow allowed herself to fall into a web of deceit, pain, abuse, and lies, disguised as love, one from which she couldn't get out so easily.

He forbade her from having a bank account and credit card. Whenever she brought it up, he would complain. He convinced her that it wasn't necessary. Instead of taking the initiative and doing what was best for her, she caved in and wallowed in her despair. How could someone as intelligent and smart as she was, allow herself to be treated in such a manner and become a pawn in Jonathan's world of lies, sex, and deceit? She was so in love with the suave, debonair, and cunning Jonathan, that she never saw the writing on the wall until it was too late.

Miles away from her family and friends, she wasn't allowed to have any acquaintances. He didn't allow her to work. She was home alone most of the time. The thought of returning to Toledo never crossed her mind. It was only when she thought about walking away, that she decided to email her mother, instead of calling and telling her that she was leaving, Jonathan. She never told her that she was heading to New York, but rather to California to start over, even as her mother pleaded with her to return home.

No longer able to deal with the physical abuse and Jonathan's other shenanigans; she took what little money she had and bought a one-way ticket to New York City. With only her clothes on her back and her documents, she walked away from Jonathan's so-called life of luxury.

***

As the rush-hour crowd pushed and bumped their way to the nearest subway station, Rain thought to herself, *there's no way in the world I'll go back to him, even if he comes after me. Hell fucking, no!* trying to suppress the bubbles her stomach was making; a despondent Rain made her way to a small eatery on the corner of Broadway and East 8th Street. As she waited by the door, a tall handsome gentleman approached. She opened the door.

"Thank you," he said, entering.

"Excuse me, sir, can you . . .?"

Cutting her off, the gentleman said, "Sure, order what it is that you want. Here take this," he smiled and handed her a twenty-dollar bill.

"Thank you," she managed to smile, her dry cracked lips now smothered with saliva as the thought of getting something to eat watered her mouth.

The gentleman ate his meal and left without saying another word. She ordered a plate of steak, eggs, and potatoes, and a large glass of orange juice. She devoured the food within minutes as the other diners eyed her with raised eyebrows. She left the eatery with six dollars in her pocket and as she headed in the direction of the Port Authority bus terminal, she bumped into a young woman whose appearance seemed to fear no better than her own. As they chatted, the conversation quickly turned to a place where she could sleep. The woman told her about a women's shelter on the Lower East Side and gave her the direction. She got on the subway. But despite the direction she was given, she had to ask several riders before getting to her destination. Unfortunately for her, she didn't know the eatery wasn't far from the shelter. She could have saved herself a few dollars.

She was given a room with two other women and given the rules. To remain at the shelter the women had to find gainful employment within a month. There was no drinking and smoking allowed on or inside the premises. Rain accepted her situation and dealt with it accordingly and in a matter of days, she found a job as a receptionist at a local doctor's office.

The doctor liked her and through a mutual friend offered her a studio apartment just across the bridge in the Williamsburg section of Brooklyn, several months later. It wasn't long before she moved in.

"I want you to be careful," the doctor said to her one afternoon.

"What do you mean?"

"Haven't you heard about the three women who were killed? Two were murdered in Manhattan by Central Park West. The other body was found in Brooklyn, but the police believed that woman was killed elsewhere."

"Yes, I saw it on the news. That is so sad."

"Be careful, the police believe it's the work of a serial killer."

"I know, but I promise you that I will be extra careful."

She hadn't thought about the murders much, but as she sat in Mario's Deli, the impact of it suddenly hit her. The woman's body was found only feet away from the Williamsburg Bridge. Her apartment was three blocks from where the body was found. The area was cordoned off by the police as the investigators tried to figure out who could have dumped the body. She was standing at the ATM, a few blocks away, and was able to see the removal of the body to the coroner's van.

It suddenly dawned on her that it could have been her under the bridge. She was cautious from that moment on. She was mindful of the fact that the murders weren't solved and that the murderer or murderers were still on the loose.

Rain knew all too well that despite the tragedies and the selfish behavior of some New Yorkers, they were down-to-earth people. New York and New Yorkers are Wall Street, the financial capital of the world. They are fashion-conscious trendsetters. Sports dominated, with masses of people from different parts of the world, a cultural melting pot. If New York accepted you as one of her own, you are a New Yorker for life.

EPISODE

2

Three years later

As the late fall wind whipped across her face, and a steady rain poured, she saw him from the corner of her eyes. Her instincts quickly took over as he walked toward her. She hastily moved closer to the curb and flagged down several taxis — they kept going. Smiling, as the rain drenched his face, and the wind blew him unsteadily, he waved at several taxis. Turning to look at him, she stepped off the curb and stood in a puddle, waving once again, when one finally came to a stop. She closed her twisted umbrella and reached for the door when he brushed past her and sat down.

"What are you doing?" she said, staring at him.

"The same thing that you're doing, I don't see your name written anywhere in here," he said sarcastically, closing his bent shape umbrella.

She was furious. She was about to curse his ass out, but the rain was pouring, and she had no time for the bullshit, as she sat next to him.

"He stopped for me. What is your problem? You're a bold ass mutha-fucka," she snapped at him, drawing the ire of the driver.

"What is the problem? Do something!" the driver said in a thick Pakistani accent.

"Did you stop for me or him?"

"Please, share the cab!" the driver begged, staring at her as if she had lost her mind.

"Take me to Hudson and Christopher Street," the young man said.

"What are you doing?"

"What do you mean what I'm doing? The man said to share so I told him where I'm going. Just make sure you have your half of the fare," he smiled.

"Don't patronize me. You don't know me!"

"Whatever!"

The driver listened as they argued. He shook his head in disbelief and smiled. It just so happened, that she was going to Christopher and Worth Street, which was two blocks from where the young man was getting off.

"Wow! What a coincidence, we are both getting off here," he said, as the taxi pulled up on the corner.

"I'm getting off here. You're going two blocks further," she snapped at him.

She paid the driver and said goodnight. She somehow managed to get her twisted umbrella open and made her way across the street but turned around just in time as he paid his half of the fare and hopped out of the cab. He turned, smiled at her, and said goodnight before entering the Starbucks on the corner. *That mutha-fucka!* she said to herself.

***

She was laughing as she walked to her apartment. Their encounter was hilarious, to say the least, and despite their little spat; she thought he was handsome. She took a shower, grabbed a bite, and sat down to watch some television. She was in a surprisingly good mood and with nothing else to do she figured she would do a little late-night writing.

Although she was several weeks behind on her latest novel, as the deadline approached, she tackled her writing with a fervor, unlike anything she had ever done up to that point. After some time, she took a break and checked her email. The publishing house wanted the complete manuscript.

She was thrilled at the good news. Her lone novel Cruel Love was self-published. So, this was a big deal. She had dreams and aspirations of becoming a successful writer and hearing from the publisher was the break she was looking for, or so she thought.

Nothing else mattered as she turned off the television and banged away at the keyboard. She wrote with passion and conviction as she sipped on green tea with a dash of Dom Perignon. It wasn't long before she was fast asleep, and within minutes she was dreaming about the young man. The dreams were erotic. She didn't know what to think or make of them when she woke up the next morning. She still had a hangover as she lazily walked to the bathroom and got in the shower. *Wow! Those were some crazy-ass dreams!* she said to herself. After getting out of the shower, she put her robe on and began fixing breakfast.

As it was an off day, she turned the television on and finished her breakfast. As she contemplated how she would spend the rest of her day, she called her job to find out if they needed anyone, and sure enough, they did.

Needing to do something with herself, and always a workaholic, it was therapeutic for her to indulge herself in whatever task confronted her, and getting up every morning to go to work, filled that need and void. This was the missing piece in a life that was filled with so much pain and self-doubt.

Rain had successfully made the transition from victim to one of triumph. Her having to live in a woman's shelter and all the other abuses she dealt with, had only built her character and made her a stronger person. This chapter of her life is about walking away from an abusive situation and having the courage to do so.

EPISODE

3

She was relentless as she went on one interview after the other. She finally landed a job with the Target Superstore chain as an assistant manager. Besides, her former boss at the doctor's office helped her out quite a bit. She had earned her degree in Interior Design from Howard University and having a college degree and not being able to put it to good use disturbed her quite a bit. And as faith would have it, things took a turn for the better, and several months later, she was hired by the designing firm, Le Chic Interior Design. She was ecstatic upon hearing the news and celebrated with several of her newfound friends.

Located at West Fifty-Third Street and Madison Avenue, in the bustling heart of mid-town Manhattan and one of the country's most prestigious and prominent interior design companies, Le Chic was careful in who they hired. So not only did it come as a surprise to her, but it also helped boost her confidence as well.

Unafraid of the new challenges, she was determined to meet them head-on. Procrastination and failure were no longer an option. She had a new lease on life and saw it as a means by which characters are built with success being the driving force behind it all. It didn't take long for her to become one of Le Chic's top designers.

She wasn't taking anything for granted. She refused to be a legend in her own mind, and this forced her to have a backup plan and that was her writing. Her first novel Cruel Love had some minor success, but she wanted very much to get signed by one of the major publishing houses.

Ironically, she has had some success as a writer, because she had heard the horror stories of how difficult it is to get into the business, which is dominated by a bunch of authors with agendas. The key she learned was to avoid those authors and try and establish a relationship with like-minded ones and publishers alike.

So many of her contemporaries had mentioned that it's who you know in the business and not necessarily what you know. She would later realize that there's some truth to it. The horror stories were plentiful and shed light on the "crab in the barrel" attitude that some in the industry have taken. She knew no one in the business and she did come across a few people who didn't want to see her succeed. Yet she did, I guess she's one of the lucky ones. But in her case, I guess you can't keep a good woman down. And this is the attitude she had, as she prepared to make a name for herself in the literary world.

***

Dressed in black business attire, Rain added just a touch of makeup to her already beautiful face. She grabbed her Bric's black shoulder strap briefcase and headed out the door. Her colleagues were surprised to see her, including her best friend, Kelly Hilton. It was business as usual, and the hours went by rather quickly.

The day was almost over when she began telling Kelly about her encounter with the stranger in the taxi, and how she fondled herself while she dreamt about him. Kelly laughed.

"Girl, I don't know what to tell you. He got to you like that?" she asked, smiling.

"I know, right? What can I say? It's crazy!"

"What would happen if you guys ran into each other again?"

"I don't know, but I don't think it will happen. I'll have a better chance of winning the lottery before I see that man again."

"Never say never, girl!"

"Come on, let's be honest! It was just a spur of the moment, a fantasy that's all."

"Sure. But your fantasy didn't stop you from crying out, 'Fuck me! Fuck me!' did it?" They both were laughing. "I guess it's more than you can say about that fool, Matt, huh?"

"You're right," Rain said, putting a finger to her lips, telling her to shush. "As for Matt, that's an understatement, to say the least."

"How is the book? Still writing?"

"Yeah, it's almost completed. And guess what?"

"What?"

"I heard from the publishing house I told you about."

"Really?"

"Yeah, they reviewed the chapters I sent them, and now they are requesting the manuscript."

"That's great news. I'm so happy for you."

"Thanks. Hopefully, things will work out."

"It will."

"I know. What are you doing later?"

"Nothing."

"Why don't you stop by tonight."

"Sure, no problem," Kelly said, getting up to retrieve her belongings.

Rain was almost home when her phone rang. It was Kelly. She wanted to know if she would work out with her later that night at the New York Sports Club, where they are both members.

"What about our date?" Rain asked, jokingly.

"What date?" she laughed. "I thought I was only coming to visit."

"Whatever."

"Are you coming?"

"Yeah, I'll meet you there."

EPISODE

4

The sports club located at Delancey, and Allen Streets in Manhattan was like a second home to the women. They worked out regularly. It wasn't long before Rain was at her locker and changing.

"Oh, you made it. I was starting to think you stood me up," Kelly said, strutting into the locker room.

"Never that, why would I? Don't you know that you're my bestie?" Rain smiled.

The women quickly got into their normal routine as their tight-fitting spandex left nothing to the imagination. While they worked out the men kept flirting with them, which was nothing new. After several minutes of fine-tuning their bodies, they decided to take a swim. Rain was leaning against the side of the pool threading the water when a voice called out, "Hi there. You in the blue bathing suit, how are you?"

Taken aback, because she couldn't get a good look at the person's face, she got out of the water and wrapped herself in her towel. As she walked towards the small group that had blocked her view, she motioned to Kelly who was at the other end of the pool talking to a male friend. "Where are you going?" Kelly yelled from the far end of the pool.

"Nowhere!" she shouted. She felt a tap on her shoulder. Startled, she turned around to see none other than the stranger with whom she had the run-in with. "Hi, and who are you and what do you want?" she managed to stutter, pretending as if she didn't recognize him.

"Gerald, Gerald Benjamin, but everybody calls me Jerry. I'm the one you had the slight mishap with a few nights ago in the cab."

She composed herself, and in no time, she was back to her snappy attitude self, "Slight? Did you say a slight mishap? It was more one-sided, selfish, and egotistical, adrenalin male testosterone bullshit."

"Wow! That was harsh," he smiled, displaying a glistening set of beautiful white teeth.

He extended his hand. She reciprocated as she thought about the whole thing and decided to let it go.

"Rain, Rain Summer, but everybody calls me, Rain."

"That was a good one! I like that," he said, laughing, "and such a beautiful name."

"Thanks."

Gerald Benjamin was the athletic type and stood six-three. Dark brown in complexion, he carried himself with a swagger that you wouldn't consider arrogant or overly egotistical. It was more confidence and self-assurance. He apologized for his behavior and said that he wanted to be friends. She told him that it was fine and that she didn't have a problem with it.

He was sharp, witty, intelligent, and charming. His eyes were on her the whole time they spoke. She knew he was trying to downplay the whole thing. But as usual, her good looks and shapely figure held his attention. Smitten, he reached into his gym bag and handed her a card.

"If you're not in a rush, how about having a cup of ice coffee with me at the Starbucks across the street?"

"I would, but I'm here with a friend. Maybe another time, no hard feelings, right?"

"No, of course not, we can do it another time."

She said she would think about it. He had a slight smile on his face, which she thought was kind of sexy. She liked it. All the freaky thoughts that she had about him came to life, and as he turned and walked away; she could tell he was packing. He had a pair of tight-fitting spandex on, the kind track stars wear, which didn't help matters either.

She knew Kelly was checking them out, and as she walked toward her, she was grinning from ear to ear. Wanting to know what happened she told her.

"That's the guy I had the run-in with."

"Him?"

"Yeah, but why the alarm?"

"He comes here all the time. He's a cutie."

"He does? I never saw him before."

"Well, he does."

Rain shrugged her shoulders, acting as if she didn't care, knowing quite well she did. She smiled as they walked to the locker room.

EPISODE

5

The eldest of two girls, Rain led an extremely comfortable life growing up in Toledo and although the sisters had different fathers, they had a close and loving relationship. Growing up, the girls attended Chapel Academy, an elite private school. They were later enrolled in Parkside middle school, and that's when Rain began noticing a change in her mother. This had a tremendous effect on their lives. Rain and Tatyana were worried about their mother's behavior. The two were inseparable. Being the oldest, Rain watched over her. Things quickly began to unravel for the family, and Marie Dubois Gordon, who was married to Rain's father, kept his last name after their divorce. She could no longer maintain the lavish lifestyle they had all been accustomed to. And despite her job as an investment banker, she took both girls to live with her mother.

Rain's grandmother lived in a middle-class neighborhood in Ludlow, Massachusetts. They went from a pampered lifestyle to one where they had to pick up behind themselves. And instead of being chauffeured to school, they had to ride on a school bus and had to travel quite a distance to get there.

Theresa's nervous breakdown is now a thing of the past, but at the time it troubled Rain greatly. Theresa never told her what caused her nervous breakdown, and she never asked. Rain believed it had everything to do with Tatyana's father; at least he visited, whereas hers rarely did.

Rain was aware of the volatile relationship between her parents, and even at such a tender age, despite what her mother said, she knew she wasn't an innocent bystander. Whenever she would ask about her father, her mother would say he walked out on her, and that she hasn't seen him since. When Rain turned six, her mother's demeanor and behavior changed. Her parents had stopped talking to each other. Their relationship was strained at this point, and Rain never heard a word about him again. She knew his name was Eric, and it was never mentioned in the household, ever.

Although she wasn't interested in finding her father, her grandmother didn't help much either. The only information her grandmother provided was his last name, which was Gordon, a name his family adopted when they arrived in America from France, instead of using their French name Fournier; and that he had family somewhere in Cherry Hills, New Jersey. Despite those setbacks, which would have discouraged others to the point of no return, her mother and grandmother did a wonderful job raising her and Tatyana.

It's not like Theresa was bankrupt and broke, quite the contrary. She still owned two apartment buildings, stocks, and bonds, and was a partner in a fledging travel agency. Albeit the family moved down a notch from the affluent lifestyle they were used to. Fluent in French, as both her parents were born in France before moving to the states, Theresa continues to socialize with the privileged black and white French upper-middle-class. Undoubtedly, she was able to sustain many of the amenities and pleasures that come with such a lifestyle.

Rain's mother and grandmother saw to it that the girls received a formidable education. Tatyana went on to graduate from Penn State. Vivacious and attractive, her five-feet-six inches body was on the slender side. Dark brown in complexion, and unmarried, she works as a senior accountant. The straightforward type, she was very outspoken.

***

Rain and Kelly had just left the Bill Bellamy concert at Radio City Music Hall when they ran into Matthew Rory on their way to the subway station.

"Hi, ladies."

"Oh, hi, Matt," both women replied.

"How is life treating you?" he said to Rain, walking off to the side.

"I'm doing great."

"That's good, what are you guys up to?"

"We just saw Bill Bellamy."

"Oh really? That's cool."

"Yup, and he was funny."

"You still work at Le Chic?"

"Yes, I do. Why?"

"Oh nothing, I was thinking that maybe I could stop by."

"Of course, you can. We might not be a couple anymore, but you're still my friend. Here's my number, give me a call."

"Cool, you're one jazzy chick, Rain," he said, kissing her on the cheek.

"That's why I spoke to you in the first place." She smiled.

Smiling, he said, "I still have my eyes on you. Bye, Rain. Bye, Kelly."

"Don't forget to call," Rain reminded him.

"Is he trying to get back with you?" Kelly asked.

"He didn't say it exactly, but knowing him, of course. Who can resist all this?" she gestured with her hands. "I gave him my number."

"You did? I bet he's happy now. You gotta stop leading him on. You know that's what you're doing, right?"

"No, I'm not. He understands. He's just being Matt that's all."

"Yeah, I guess, and whatever you did to that fool, it's working." Both women laughed, as they got on the train.

"I believe you have led both sexes on, more so than me."

"Maybe, you think I did?" Kelly giggled.

"Yeah."

"Oh, how is Tatyana?"

"You haven't spoken to her? She's fine."

"No, the last time we spoke was about two months ago."

"Well, you need to call her then."

"I will," she said, as the train roared through the tunnel.

***

Rain met with Jerry in Starbucks as planned. He wasn't the jerk that she thought he was. He was very polite and had a great sense of humor. A bachelor, he was a graduate of Yale University.

"So, you were born and raised in Maryland?" she asked.

"Yeah, and after I received my master's, I moved to Washington, DC, but things didn't quite work out as I thought. And so, I packed my belongings and headed here. But my family lives here, I just went away to school. There's a saying that goes 'If you can make it here, you can make it anywhere' and that's the motto I have lived by ever since."

"That's a great way of looking at things. You sound quite comfortable with who you are and what you want out of life."

"Isn't that the only way to look at it?"

"Yeah, you're right. What do you do? I mean, you did graduate from Yale."

"I work in stocks and bonds and securities, alongside my father on Wall Street. We have clients all over the world."

"All over the world?"

"That's right! You name it, we'll have it. Whether it's Paris, Rome, Istanbul, Hong Kong, London, Saudi Arabia, or Nigeria, if we can't get it done then no one can."

"Wow!" She was about to get the absolute shock of her life.

"Are you familiar with the name, Herbert Benjamin?"

"I think so."

"Well, that's my father."

"Really!" she had believed everything that he said up to that point. *But this was going too far*, she thought.

His father was Wall Street millionaire, Herbert Benjamin. She was in total disbelief. She thought he was lying. As far as she was concerned, so what, they shared the same last name. It wasn't until he pulled out his cellphone and showed her a photo of them together did her doubts began to wane. She had never been in the company of anyone who was related to someone famous, much less an influential icon who was known not only on Wall Street but all over the world. She figured she had to say something about herself but didn't know where to start. Yet some tell-tale signs about the elder Benjamin shook her.

Sensing that she was somewhat hesitant, he asked, "Are you originally from New York City?"

"Who me?" she asked, pointing at herself.

"Yeah, you!" he answered, smiling as they burst out laughing.

"No. I'm from Michigan."

"Detroit?"

"No, Bloomfield Hills."

"For a second there, I thought you were Motown. You know, Smokey Robinson, Diana Ross, Marvin Gaye, and The Temptations. Berry Gordy was the man!"

"Yes, he was, and don't forget about the Jackson Five."

"How could I, what made you move to New York?"

After explaining she was originally from Toledo, Florida, and later moved to Michigan, she told him she was thinking about pursuing a modeling career upon graduating from college. She decided not to say anything about her marriage and why she moved to Michigan.

She felt it wasn't time for her to share those details.

"So, the modeling thing drove you here, huh?"

"Yup! I didn't come immediately though."

"Why not? What stopped you?"

"Miami."

"How so?"

"I was living in Florida after I graduated and so I thought that maybe if I moved to Miami, I could get in the business."

"I see, but I thought Miami was a good place to get in the business, isn't it?"

"How many models do you know of or heard of that got their start in Miami? The numbers are very low."

"Yeah, you're right. It's California and New York."

"You're so right, and at that stage of my life, I didn't want to travel to either place. Besides, my life was pretty complicated back then."

"What do you mean by complicated?" he inquired, smiling.

"I'll tell you one day," she said, returning his smile.

"I'm going to keep you to your word."

"Sure, but as I was saying, it was too much, and look at me, I wasn't thin enough."

"You look fine to me. You don't need to lose anything," his eyes looked her over.

She smiled and continued, "After endless auditions and not getting anywhere I thought about enrolling in graduate school at my alma mater."

"Where did you do your undergraduate studies?"

"Howard."

"That's great! It's an excellent school. Seems like you were all over the country, huh? So, you're an interior designer?"

"Yes. I'm also a writer."

"Are you serious? Wow!"

"Yes."

"What genre do you write, romance, urban, erotica, fiction, non-fiction, what?"

"Fiction, erotica, and romance."

"Hmm," he smiled. "Do you have anything out right now?"

"Yeah, it's called Cruel Love."

"I'll have to pick that up."

"That'll be nice and let me know what you think. While you're at it, you can also check out the Write Lover by my good friend, Brooklen Borne."

"I'll do that. Oh, and you're how old again?"

"I never told you," she smiled. "But if you insist . . ."

"I'm insisting," he said, cutting her off.

Giggling, she said, "I'm twenty-five."

He smiled and said, "How come I don't believe you."

"Well, you know a lady never tells her age, but I'm closer to you than you think. And how old are you?" she smiled.

"I'm thirty."

"See, I told you I was close to your age," she giggled.

"I guess I'll wait until you're willing to share your secrets," he squinted at her.

They both agreed that 2006 was a special year. He told her things were going great, and she felt the same. They had a warm and friendly conversation. He seemed impressed with the things she said. The whole time he was smiling, his eyes were glued to her face and body, and he made it known. He convinced her to go with him to the Brooklyn Museum of Art. It was a wonderful experience as they poked fun at each other and agreed to see each other again.

She was on cloud nine when she got home. She called Kelly and told her how the date went. Kelly screamed as if she was the one who went on the date. She was happy for Rain and reminded her to keep her eyes on the ring; the wedding ring that is. Rain said she would. This was something the two talked about all the time, getting their man.

After hanging up the phone, Rain poured herself a glass of Krug and turned the computer on. She typed one erotic scene after the other. But the more she wrote, the more turned on she was, and the alcohol had her going in circles. No longer able to control her desires, she retrieved her dildo from the night table drawer and pleasured herself.

EPISODE

6

Friends are difficult to come by, and Rain and Kelly are living proof of this. After becoming friends, the two would make their weekend rendezvous on the Lower East Side and Upper West Side of Manhattan, partying. Tatyana would go along with them whenever she was in town. Kelly and Tatyana would soon become fast friends.

Kelly's life was filled with turmoil as well, and she had experienced more than her share of dysfunctional relationships. Divorced, she went through a nasty breakup with her then-husband. Married for four years and having to experience the tragic death of her daughter at the age of two, almost drove her to a nervous breakdown. The following two years of her marriage were tumultuous. Her husband was nothing more than a functional alcoholic, abuser, and womanizer.

With her striking good looks, shoulder-length brown hair, and shapely figure, she was every man and woman's dream. It was only when her husband's infidelity overwhelmed her that she began an affair with a childhood female friend of hers.

Dressed in blue designer jeans and a matching top, she entered the room. Her expensive designer glasses perched on her nose hid her striking brown eyes. She ignored the small group of men staring at her and entered Samantha Jennings's office. An advertising executive, she was happy to see her. The two women immediately began talking.

"I don't know how much longer I can deal with this," Kelly said to her.

"Is he still coming around, harassing you?"

"Yes, he is, and I'm beyond fed up. I want his ass as far away from me as possible."

"Well, we are going to have to figure something out."

"It had better be soon because I can't take this anymore." She was upset.

Getting up, the two friends embraced and kissed the other softly on the cheek. Samantha reassured her that things would work out for the better, but unfortunately, they didn't.

***

She made a fatal mistake by going to his apartment, which her friends had warned her about. He wanted her to take him back, but she refused. He was getting angrier the more she explained her reason for not wanting him back. Frustrated, he grabbed her by the arm.

"Please stop! It hurts!" she cried. He placed his huge hand over her mouth. He mounted her removing his pants and underwear in one motion. Using his knees, he spread her legs apart and penetrated her.

"Stay still," he growled in a drunken stupor, moving his hips in a circular motion, and breathing heavily. She screamed as he forced himself deep inside her. He was hurting her.

Her screams didn't matter as she begged him to stop. Instead, he pinned her on the bed and continued to violate her. Her body shuddered. She was aroused strangely and shamelessly. His pace quickened as he was about to cum. His weight was overbearing, and as she screamed, he thought it was being done to give him immense pleasure.

"See, doesn't this feel much better?" he said.

"Yeah," she stammered, terrified. She only said it so he would hurry up and get it over with.

She was at a loss for words. She was in shock. But he kept rambling about how she was a whore, and he was going to treat her like one. All she could think of were the rapes and the beatings, and she blamed herself for believing him and showing up. She remained still, and although she felt some pain her body responded as if it had a mind of its own.

She felt a tremendous amount of guilt and that bothered her. She closed her eyes. She didn't know what to think or do, as her mind and body struggled to make sense of all that was happening. The stench of marijuana and alcohol reeked on his breath. His moans were eerie and frightening to her. She couldn't recall how long he abused her, but she was relieved when it was over.

"I will kill you if you ever fucking report this."

"I won't," she nodded, scared. She got up and left the room.

She didn't dare tell anyone, not even her family or closest friends. She kept quiet as he told her. It had gotten to the point where she feared being home alone.

EPISODE

7

Alonzo Hilton was a handsome and powerfully built man. He stood six feet four in height. A finance officer for the state of New York, he was heading up the corporate ladder. Encouraged by his peers and considered a "wiz kid" by his superiors, he knew it was only a matter of time before he gets the promotion he craves. But unbeknownst to everyone, was his drinking problem. They knew he drank, but not to the extent he would in private. It wasn't long before his life began spiraling out of control.

Unaware of this, a smitten Kelly fell head over heels in love with him. She accompanied him on his many trips to upstate Albany, where he was assigned at times. Kelly loved it. She mingled with many of the state's powerbrokers and welcomed the attention. They were in love with each other and when Alonzo proposed, she didn't hesitate to say yes.

It wasn't long before they were married and immediately following the honeymoon, the beatings began. Afraid and embarrassed, she refused to tell anyone. The black eyes were hidden by dark glasses and the bruises on her body were hidden by pants and long sleeve blouses. The lies mounted and when confronted by friends and family members they were told it was none of their business.

Alonzo began coming home late and when she questioned him, he ignored her. She no longer accompanied him to Albany, and he would be gone for weeks at a time. She knew he was cheating, but she was in denial. After confronting him about their marriage and whether he still loved her, he wouldn't talk about it. This went on for weeks before he surprised her one evening with flowers, dinner, and champagne at one of New York City's finest five-star restaurants.

In Kelly's mind, things were back to normal or so it seemed. He showered her with lots of expensive gifts. His late-night escapades were now a thing of the past. And when she told her friends and family that she was pregnant, they were happy for her. Yet they had their doubts. Nonetheless, they took it for what it was worth. She was happy and that was all that mattered.

Confident that Alonzo was willing to work on their marriage, especially with a baby on the way; Kelly was devastated when he picked up where he left off. Things got so bad that she requested more hours at her job to pay the bills. Somehow, she managed to make ends meet. Alonzo's drinking and womanizing eventually led to his firing. Without a steady source of income, he sold over-the-counter prescription pills and whatever else he got his hands on. With the birth of their daughter, she thought this would motivate him to change his lifestyle, instead, things only got worse. The beating continued and sadly the death of their daughter is what eventually drove her to file for divorce.

Kelly had to pick up a few items from the supermarket and left Alonzo with the baby. High on pills, the baby somehow ended up in the backyard and managed to crawl into their neighbor's pool and drown. Sadly, it was deemed an accident, and Alonzo was never charged. Kelly stood by him after the baby's death, but the only thing that mattered to him was drugs, drinking, money, and pussy; and when he was no longer able to get his drugs at his old hangouts, he began stealing from Kelly's friends and family. When they refused to support his habit, he threatened them. One night after partying, drinking, and smoking, he got into an argument with Kelly's mother. To everyone's surprise, he pulled out a gun and pointed it in her face; all the while screaming that he would kill her. After calming him down, Kelly begged her mother and friends not to call the police. She breathed a sigh of relief when they agreed not to.

***

Several days later, Kelly got the shock of her life. She was on her lunch break with two of her female co-workers when they were approached by Alonzo, shockingly enough, he was sober. Frightened, the women panicked. They were about to run when he quickly cornered them.

"What the fuck do you want?" Kelly screamed at him.

"I miss you and I want you back . . ."

"You miss me, and you want me back? Do you think that's how it works? Do you think you can say you want me back and it's so? Are you outta your fucking mind?" Her co-workers looked on with raised eyebrows.

"Why can't we reconcile and work out our differences?"

"Are you fucking crazy, reconcile what? You need to move on with your life."

"The divorce isn't finalized. We can work things out."

"Work what out? Get away from me!"

"Get away from her! Leave her alone, you fucking ass!" one of her co-workers snapped.

"You think I don't know about that guy you're seeing? You have no respect for me," he rambled on.

"Respect? Listen, I will see whoever the fuck I want and whenever I want."

"The fuck you won't."

"You know what Alonzo, go?"

"I'm not going anywhere until I'm done with you."

"Really?" as if on cue the women began screaming at him.

"I'm going to deal with the two of you. You just wait and see."

The commotion quickly caught the ears of several people who were also on their lunch break. Faced with the threat of the police showing up at any moment, he bolted for the subway. He was fuming as he got on the train. He vowed that he would make her pay. Not only did he blame her for the break-up of their marriage, but he also blamed her for the death of their daughter.

"You have to be careful," her other co-worker said. "That mutha-fucka is crazy! He's a fucking psycho!"

"I know," she replied. "I don't know what's wrong with him. It had been a while since I last saw him."

"This mutha-fucka just pops up out of nowhere saying he wants to get back with you, what the fuck!" the other woman said.

"He's been harassing me of late and now that the divorce is in process, he's been on my ass."

"You need to hurry up and finalize the divorce."

"That's what I'm trying to do."

"Just be careful," both women advised her.

It wasn't long before the divorce was finalized. Kelly, her family, and close friends were thrilled that it was over with.

EPISODE

8

With her divorce finalized, Kelly breathed a sigh of relief, thinking the worst was behind her. Unfortunately, it wasn't, but she took it for what it was worth and was prepared to face an unknown future. She moved in with her new boyfriend and was hired by Le Chic. It was a new start, and she had an optimistic outlook on life. What she didn't know was that Samantha didn't like the idea of her moving in with her new boyfriend. The two spoke and decided to meet up later that evening. They met in Union Square and walked the short walk to one of the outside cafés in the West Village.

"Who is that guy everyone says they have seen you with? Is he the guy you moved in with?" Samantha asked.

"Yeah and . . .?"

"Why would you move in with him without saying anything to me?"

"I didn't know I had to report to you?"

"I thought you and I were seeing each other."

"I never said anything of the sort. You chose to believe that."

"So, you were fucking with me, is that it?"

"I was not fucking with you. What is wrong with you?"

"Everything!"

"Samantha, enough is enough."

"No, you are wrong."

"I'm not wrong. We weren't dating."

"So, you're fucking him?"

"What type of dumb-ass question is that? Is this why you invited me here for this bullshit? You know what, I'm leaving."

"Don't walk away from me."

Kelly left like she said, as a pissed Samantha ran after her, but it was to no avail. Samantha hadn't heard from her in almost a month. Kelly refused her calls, emails, and Facebook and Twitter messages. Irate, Samantha began stalking the couple. Unaware of this, Kelly continued her normal routine until one afternoon she decided to respond to Samantha's text message. The women reconciled their differences and had lunch at Bar Boulud, a French restaurant on the Upper West Side. Staring at her as they spoke, Kelly took a sip of her drink and said, "Samantha at times you scare me. You do."

Samantha had a slight smirk on her face as she got up from her seat and rubbed Kelly's cheek. "I would never do anything to harm or hurt you. You mean the world to me." Kelly smiled.

***

Samantha was under the impression that she and Kelly were going to rekindle their relationship. She was outraged when Kelly rebuffed her advances. Also, Kelly hadn't been coming around like she normally did. This didn't sit well at all with her. Pissed, she confronted her.

"Why haven't you been coming around of late?"

"I just need some space that's all."

"Space? From who, me? Ever since you moved in with that fucker you have been acting like a bitch . . ."

"Oh, so now I'm a bitch, huh? That's how you feel about me?"

"No, I didn't mean it that way."

"Then what did you mean, Samantha? Please enlighten me."

"You know what I meant."

"No, I don't."

"You know what? Okay, I'm sorry. But it doesn't take away from the fact that you don't come around like you used to."

"I told you. I need some me-time. What is your problem?"

"You! You are my problem."

"You're not going to do this to me. You're not going to treat me like this, fuck no, no!"

"Treat you how, huh?"

"Listen, if we are going to be friends then be my friend. But you are not going to tell me who to see and how to live my life."

"Look at how you're treating me."

"You're a fucking self-centered, egotistical, and bipolar bitch."

"What? Oh, that's how you feel about me? Huh? How dare you disrespect me in such a manner?"

"Because I'm fucking tired of your bullshit!"

"Okay, I'm sorry! I'm fucking sorry. It's just that I feel like I'm losing you and I don't know how to handle it. You fault me for that?"

"No, but you could have been more considerate."

"You're right. Let's go over to my place and have a drink and talk about it."

"Samantha, we can walk the two blocks to our usual spot and have a drink."

"Okay, fair enough."

As the women drank, Kelly was still pissed and refused to divulge any information about her boyfriend.

***

Kelly's boyfriend was on his way home late one night when he noticed a black Nissan Murano tailing him. It was only the blaring sirens from two speeding fire trucks that enabled him to get away from the pursuing Murano. He downplayed the whole thing as just a car heading in the direction that he was. He had a few close calls but became unnerved when he began noticing a parked car across the street from his office. When he finally built up his nerves and approached the car, no one was in it. He kept it to himself before sharing it with Kelly. She was stunned and wanted to know why he took so long to bring it to her attention.

"At first I thought nothing of it," he explained. "But soon thereafter, it became unbearable. Something isn't right."

"Of course, it's not. Did you notice anything that might be of help?"

"No, not really! I thought I saw a black girl with blonde hair following me about a week ago."

"Really?"

"Yeah, she was about your height, a bit thicker, but that's all I could make out."

"Hmm, strange."

"What is it?"

"Oh, nothing, I was just thinking about something."

"Do you know about any of what's happening?"

"My friend Samantha, the one I told you about?"

"Yeah, what about her?"

"At times she can get pretty irrational."

"Irrational, how?"

"She does a lot of dumb shit."

"Oh?"

"Yes."

"Hmm. I see."

She filled him in on Samantha and what she thought about her. "On another note, Alonzo keeps showing up at my mother's house."

"He does?"

"Yes, and I am worried."

"This guy is a jerk and needs to be locked up. He needs an ass-kicking."

"I'm getting sick of his shit."

"The cops will deal with his ass sooner rather than later."

"I hope so."

***

The next day, Kelly decided to visit Samantha at her workplace. She had an uncomfortable look on her face as Kelly entered.

"What brings you here?" she asked

"You know."

"What do I know?"

"My boyfriend. You're the one who has been following him."

"How dare you come into my office and accuse me of such things? You know what . . ."

"Go ahead and deny it, Samantha, go ahead."

"How can you say such things about me?"

"Is it true or not? I will go to the police."

"Get outta my fucking office, you ungrateful bitch. I looked after your dumb ass when that no-good bastard husband of yours was beating your ass and made you lose your child. It was me. It wasn't any of your so-called friends or your man, it was me. So how dare you come into my office, accusing me of shit you have no proof of, and you want me to tell you something to make you feel good? Get the fuck out!"

"I will, you fucking bitch. But you're gonna pay if it's you. I knew you were a sick fuck . . ."

"Get the fuck out! Get out!"

Kelly had voiced her concerns to her two co-workers about Samantha's behavior. They warned her that it wasn't a good idea to be around her and that she was a ticking time bomb.

***

It was a lonely strip about twelve miles from Jones Beach. It was sometime after eight o'clock on a Saturday night that the body was found lying in a ditch. It was the body of a female. She was shot multiple times. There was no sign of a struggle. The police immediately ruled out robbery. The deceased was Samantha Jennings. Upon hearing the news, Kelly was stunned. She was speechless. She certainly didn't wish such an outcome on her childhood friend.

If she thought things were going to get any better, she was wrong. Three weeks later, Alonzo's bullet-riddled body was found several feet from the Fulton Fish Market in the Hunts Point section of the Bronx, where he worked. According to the witnesses that the police spoke to, a lone gunman with a hoodie over his head approached the deceased as he was getting in his car and pumped several bullets into his body. The killer then fled in a car. The eyewitnesses couldn't make out the license plates or the make of the car.

The murder of Samantha and Alonzo wasn't something Kelly could easily overlook. Despite the roller-coaster ups and downs between the two, she wanted to know why they were killed, and who did it. She made it a priority to stay in contact with the police.

EPISODE

9

A young woman was held and brutally tortured before being murdered and dumped in Central Park, the evening news reporter said. The dead woman's friend, a victim herself, is lucky to be alive. The young woman whose name is being withheld told the police there was a knock on her door and recognizing her friend, she opened it, only to be confronted by a masked man with a gun. Both women were quickly hog-tied, assaulted, and sodomized for several hours.

Rain was speechless as she sat watching the television. The deprived and deviant acts were part of a sadistic and horrific conundrum of power and control, the reporter continued. The victims had burns on their bodies and other physical damages, including broken bones. The women were threatened repeatedly with death and were beaten continuously and mercilessly.

According to police investigators, "the woman said her friend was taken from the bedroom to the bathroom and that's where she saw her lifeless body. After a few more hours of raping her, she said she felt something cold on her neck. She cannot recall exactly what happened next, but she does remember being inside the trunk of a car and feeling the thorns, dirt, and bushes as she and her friend were dumped in the park."

Scarred and bandaged as she lay in the hospital, the ghastly ordeal was still on her mind as the memory of her sadistic and degenerate abuser paralyzed her with fear. It was traumatic for her to talk at times.

"I thought I was dead. I'm so happy to be alive. He wanted to kill me, for what I don't know," she cried to the investigators.

"You are safe now," one of them replied, comforting her.

The deprived act stunned law enforcement officials and the city. The degree of brutality was unlike anything they had ever seen one police investigator said.

The murder and assault were on Rain's mind the next day at work. And much to her dismay, the whole office was talking about it. Kelly, who lived not too far from where the bodies were dumped, was worried.

"Just be careful," Rain warned her.

"I will. There were a lot of cops patrolling the park and the nearby streets when I left for work this morning, so that's good. I just hope they keep it up."

"I think they will."

"But didn't they find some bodies in the park some time ago?"

"They did, but . . ."

"It means they are fucking up."

"I don't think so. Maybe this guy is picking his spots. You know what I mean?"

"Well, they better hurry up and find whoever is doing this shit. I'm freaking scared. At least you live on the east side."

"So, do you wanna come and stay with me until you feel better?"

"I'm gonna wait and see first. Is that okay with you?"

"Sure!"

"Oh, before I forget, I was invited to a party next week and I want you to come with me."

"Of course, where is it?"

"By 59th and Columbus Circle!"

"It's a date."

***

Matthew was convinced that it was their final lover's spat, which was the cause of his and Rain's breakup. For months, he pleaded with her to give him another chance, but she would have none of it. What he failed to realize was that the relationship had run its course. Being stuck in a passionless marriage for several years, Rain knew the warning signs and although the two were only boyfriend and girlfriend, she wasn't going to take that chance. Matthew was deeply hurt.

Born and raised in Philadelphia, Matthew stood six-one in height. The athletic type, he's handsome, outgoing; and a graduate of Drexel University. For as long as Matthew could remember, he had always wanted the ideal American family, the house with the picket fence, wife, and children. In his mind, it was what most Americans wanted, or so he thought until he encountered several women with whom he had several memorable relationships. They didn't aspire to or desire the things that he wanted in life. Their relationships were filled with lies, infidelity, and a total lack of respect for each other. Matthew's love life was spiraling out of control, but fortunately for him, he saw the warning signs and moved on.

It wasn't until he met Rain that he did a self-evaluation of himself. He fell madly in love the moment he laid eyes on her. He was more than thrilled when they began dating. But he had some issues that he had to deal with. He had become very brash, uncompromising, conceited, and stubborn. He blamed his ways on his past relationships. With Rain, he had found someone who was the opposite of the women in his past. For a long time, he was unsure of how to express himself early on in their relationship. He was quite the charismatic type before the other women and he longed to become his old self once again, and Rain did that. She gave new meaning to his life. She brought sunshine to his cloudy days. His love for others had grown cold and a new day for him seemed old. She brightened up his days and the struggles he faced became a thing of the past.

She entered his life and changed not only his temperament but his whole outlook on life and love. She taught him how to express his love and, how to rid himself of his fears and learn to love the person that he is. Her love for him was unconditional and filled with promise. However, Matthew had a narcissistic streak and unfortunately, it led to their breaking up; the first of many. It had finally hit rock bottom. Left with no other option, Rain ended it for good. She had enough.

The years they were together were tumultuous, to say the least. He says he was convinced that it was her friends rather than any hindrance on his part for their breakup. There was more to it than that. Oddly enough, he saw himself as a victim. The false misconception he had about their relationship was created in part, because of his staying out late and his womanizing ways, which Rain wanted no part of.

He was at home when he decided to call Rain. It had been some time since they last spoke.

"Hi."

"Hi, how are you?"

"Not so great, things have been kind of difficult."

"What do you mean? What's going on?"

"I lost my job, and the bills are piling up."

"It's that bad?"

"Yeah!"

"Why didn't you say something?"

"I don't know."

"I could have said a few words on your behalf at Le Chic, they are hiring."

"I should have . . . but they are?"

"Yes . . . tell you what; I'll see what I can do."

"Are you serious?"

"Yes, I'm serious."

"Thank you so much, Rain. It would mean the world to me."

"Don't worry about it. I know you would have done the same for me."

"You know I would."

"Great. I'll keep you posted."

"Thanks, Rain, bye."

EPISODE

10

It was the weekend of the party and as planned the women met up and took the short ride by subway. Rain wanted to know who invited Kelly.

"Who you said it was again?"

"A writer friend told me about it," Kelly said.

"Is the friend here?"

"Oh, no, she couldn't make it. But there are several people here that I know, because of her, of course."

"I see."

"Why, is something wrong?"

"No. I needed to get out of the house, and since Jerry was busy, I thought, why not have some innocent fun with my girl."

"Innocent? Girl, please," they laughed.

They were enjoying themselves when they were approached by the handsome and suave, Jordan Jagger. A thirty-seven-year-old journalist, writer, author, and a known reveler on the Manhattan party scene, he was quite the character. Standing well over six feet, he had his eyes on Rain, the minute she arrived.

"Hi, Kelly? Who is your friend?" he asked. Stunned, she was at a loss for words. She wasn't quite expecting this. Rain was surprised, to say the least.

"Oh, hi Jordan, this is, Rain."

"Nice meeting you."

"Likewise," he said, "care to dance?"

Rain took him up on the offer. After telling her what he did for a living, her phone rang. She excused herself and took the call.

"Who was that? Was that your boyfriend?" he asked.

She glared at him before saying, "So, how long have you been writing, and what are the titles of your books?"

"Cry, Never Loved, Stormy Nights, Alone, and Lost!"

"Those are some rather interesting titles."

"They are, right? But you never answered my question."

"What question?"

"The call."

"Isn't that a bit presumptuous, asking me this?"

"You're right. I apologize." She gazed at him as he continued. "Getting back to what I was saying, what I always try and do is to give my readership a cover that will enthrall and take their imagination to some forbidden place. Usually, a place where they can reflect on what it is that they are going through at that particular moment, and hopefully once they start reading, that forbidden place or thing will come to life through my writing."

"Wow! That's very thoughtful, nicely put."

"Why thank you! And what are the names of your titles?"

"Titles? No!" she laughed. "I have only published one book, Cruel Love, and I'm presently finishing up, A Lost Soul." She was surprised he knew she was a writer. *It must have been Kelly,* she thought.

Smiling, he said, "Hey, one is better than none, and you're finishing book two, so that's great."

"Thank you."

"Here's my card, and I'm sorry for asking such a personal question. I was out of place. Can you forgive me?"

"Sure, it's nothing." She took the card.

"Have you done any book signings, shows, or anything like that?"

"No, I haven't."

"What about marketing?"

"Not too much, because I have been busy working and taking care of other things."

"I understand, but if you want to make a mark in this business, you have to do all the necessaries that I mentioned and then some."

"You got that right!" she laughed.

"Look, give me a call and I can set up a signing for you at the Barnes and Noble at Fifth Avenue and 18th Street."

"You can?" she asked, ecstatic. "Oh, my God, that's awesome, Jordan."

"Hey, we are all writers, right?"

"Yeah, that's so cool."

"Think nothing of it."

Rain was taken by his vast knowledge of the publishing business despite his barefaced approach. She felt he was someone that could be of great help. After their conversation, she pulled Kelly aside.

"I saw the look on your face when you saw him. Where do you know him from?"

"He's a good friend. We have known each other for some time now. Of course, I was surprised to see him. It's not every day you're invited to a party, and you meet someone from your past. The last time we spoke he was living in California. I didn't even know he was a writer."

"So, you didn't tell him I was a writer?"

"No. I'm just as surprised now, hearing it from you."

"Oh, wow!"

"Believe me, I didn't."

"I believe you."

"Does it matter if he said it?"

"No. I was just curious," Rain said, moving on.

"Shit, I was surprised when I saw him?"

"Yeah, I saw the look."

"I bet you did."

"Is he a cool dude?"

"From what I know, yeah."

"That's good because he knows a lot about the writing and book business and he's willing to help me."

"That's great but be careful. You saw how he looked at you."

"I saw it. But trust me, it won't happen."

"Good. I like that. There are some things I have to tell you about him, but here is not the place."

"Okay. Is it bad?"

"No, it's not."

Before Rain could respond, Jordan approached. She left them alone. She was getting acquainted with the other guests when she noticed them looking in her direction. She thought nothing of it. Besides, it didn't hurt that the two were good friends.

***

Rain and Jerry began seeing more of each other and it wasn't long before she began questioning their relationship. Unsure of how he would react and how it would affect him if she were to tell him that she was still married, she decided it wouldn't be a good idea. It certainly didn't help either as she found herself becoming more dependent on him. In this case, it had nothing to do with her finances or holding her hostage in the relationship. It was more about needing someone to confide in and call in her time of need. However, because of the complicated life she led with Jonathan, she would at times withdraw, for fear of not being good enough or being equal, and that at times was troubling.

Rain's life was a paradox, filled with inconsistency, insecurities, and a mindset of not being good enough to measure up. Yet in the same breath, she was articulate, poise, eloquent, intelligent, and loving. Nonetheless, it seemed as if she needed someone in her life to take charge more or less. And although Jerry was the opposite of Jonathan Banks and cared for her, at times she wanted nothing to do with their relationship, and the next minute she craved it. This was something she vowed would never happen again. Even so, it was much too late, when she finally realized how far she had allowed herself to get involved.

"Rain, I know things have been moving rather quickly between us, but make no mistake about it, I'm here for the long haul. This isn't about a short-term relationship. I see beyond that. I know there are some things that you haven't shared with me. I'm not going to harass you about it.

When you think the time is right to share it with me, do so," Jerry said to her in a quiet voice as they talked over dinner.

"Okay. Oh, there's so much I need to tell you and say, but at this moment, I need to reevaluate my life and certain occurrences that took place. I just want to be free from any ridicule that I may have shown so far, but . . ."

Cutting her off in mid-sentence, he said, "No, stop it; I would never ridicule you no matter what. I'm here to listen. I'm not here to judge you. I'm a willing listener."

"There's something I need to ask you."

"Sure, go ahead."

"It's been six months since we have been seeing each other and you haven't forced yourself on me. Even after I explained to you that at times, I get horny, I wanted to wait, because I didn't want to rush into a situation where I might end up getting hurt. You never pushed the issue, why?"

"I respect you as a person and as a woman. I was brought up to respect others' wishes, just as I would like them to respect mine. Words cannot describe how I feel about you. I'm a man and a real man should respect his woman's wishes. Of course, I'm dying to make love to you, but I'll wait until you're ready."

Giggling, because of how he said those last few words, Rain added, "I want you too. I do. You wouldn't like to know what I do when I get horny."

"Try me, go ahead. Oh, let me guess, you use one of those things?"

"Me and my big mouth, I'm so embarrassed," she giggled.

"Embarrass for what?"

"Okay, okay, yeah, I use one," she said, laughing."

"Nothing is wrong with that; you did what you had to do to relieve yourself."

"Oh, my God, relieve? Wow!" she continued laughing. There was a romantic spark and silence as they stared into each other's eyes. Jerry's hands slowly moved across the table and held hers.

"Are you ready?"

"Yes," she replied.

It was the moment they had both been waiting for. But was it? She was filled with guilt because of how close they had become. She felt terrible. She began to think that maybe it wasn't such a good idea to keep her marriage hidden from him. Jonathan had not filed for divorce and neither had she. And whenever the topic of marriage came up, she answered as honestly as she could. Whether she was right or wrong in taking such a stance, was something that she would later find out.

EPISODE 11

Rain and Kelly were curious about how Matthew's interview with Le Chic turned out. He was a great interviewer but not knowing the outcome was on her mind.

"Didn't Matt have an interview today?" Kelly asked Rain.

"He sure did."

"I wonder how it went."

"He'll let us know."

"Okay. Are you ready to go?"

"Yeah, they worked my ass off today. I was supposed to have dinner with Jerry tonight, but I'll invite him over because I'm way too tired. Doubt if I'll do any writing."

"You know damn well you won't be doing any writing."

"I'll probably hear from him soon," she giggled.

"Once Jerry is there, nothing gets done. Who are you trying to fool, yourself?" They burst out in laughter.

The ringing of Rain's phone interrupted their conversation.

"Hi, Rain."

"Hi, Matt!"

"I have good news. They hired me."

"That's wonderful!" she yelled, "and Kelly says congratulations."

"Tell her I said, hi!"

They continued their conversation as Rain made her way home. Matthew said he would start training that coming Monday, and that he would be in her department. She thought a lot about Matthew and considered him a great friend. But as usual, the conversation soon turned to him getting back with her, which she wanted no part of. He wanted to know if he could stop by her apartment. The answer was a polite no. She then ended the conversation.

***

When Jerry arrived, Rain was dressed and ready to go. Puzzled, he wanted to know why she had changed her mind.

"I had second thoughts about staying home. I know what I said, but I . . ."

"Baby, it's okay. I understand. Your wish is my command." She smiled as they walked to the elevator.

They had a wonderful time at one of New York's finest restaurants. After dinner, they went back to her apartment where they cuddled and watched television. As she lay in his arms, she imagined how things would have turned out if she weren't menstruating. It wasn't long before they fell asleep. They had a wonderful weekend together.

***

He preyed on his victim's kindness, fear, vulnerability, trustworthiness, and passiveness. A loner, he struck several times, baffling police investigators who initially thought he had an accomplice. He frequented the Central Park and Gramercy Park area, and now and then the Lower East Side of Manhattan. He was methodical in choosing his victims. They were mostly professionals, educated, and of all races; but the one thing they shared, and which set off a red flag for police investigators was that they all had long dark hair.

The investigators weren't convinced that he knew his victims. Nearly all the women were attacked after getting dropped off by friends. Some were followed from their place of work, the neighborhood bars, the subway, and other hangouts. Others were followed and attacked while jogging or walking in Central Park. Two were assaulted after giving him access to their buildings, where he followed and pounced upon them as they entered their apartment. The police were able to establish that his last victim was attacked after a night out with her co-workers.

In his most recent attack, he followed his victim as she left a bar after a night of drinking with friends. As the young woman fumbled for her keys, he inched closer. Stumbling as she opened the door to her apartment, he grabbed her from behind, shoving her inside. Grabbing her by the throat, he began choking and punching her, muffling her screams. The more she cried the angrier he became.

"Stop crying," he said in an almost childlike voice.

"Okay, okay," she sobbed, trying to make sense of why he attacked her. "You don't have to do this."

"Do what?"

"Rape me!"

"I don't wanna rape you," he screamed at her, tying her up.

"If it's money you want, there's five-hundred dollars in my purse and you can have the PIN to my bank card. There's also jewelry in the bedroom."

He had a menacing look on his face. He paced angrily as she continued talking. He approached her, stared into her eyes, and suddenly sat down; only to jump to his feet, telling her that she caused it on herself.

"Cause what?" she sobbed.

Smiling, he said, "You know what you did."

"What? What did I do?"

"The bar!"

"What about the bar?"

"You shouldn't have gone there," he smirked.

"Okay, I won't go there anymore. I'll do what you say. I promise. Okay, okay! No more!"

"You promise?" he said innocently.

"I promise. I won't go there anymore."

"So, you're gonna be a good girl from now on?"

"Yes! What should I call you? You do have a name, right?" she asked him, as he slowly rubbed his face against hers. He didn't answer. She cringed. "Don't you have a name? My name is Kirsten. It says it on my driver's license. You see it?"

"Kirsten, that's a pretty name. Such a pretty name for a pretty girl and you ruined it. You ruined it. How could you ruin such a pretty name? You are undeserving of it, you bitch. You're a bitch!" Stunned, she was paralyzed with fear.

Snatching her by the neck, he choked her until she was unresponsive. He removed her clothes and stood over her lifeless body, admiring his work and how peaceful she looked. Moving quickly, he cleaned his prints from the apartment. It was only the ringing of her cell phone that prompted him to leave the apartment.

***

He was unsettled as he paced inside his apartment. Finally, he undressed and got in the shower. Minutes later, he turned the television on and sat in the corner staring into the mirror.

'Who do they think they are? They aren't as important as me. They caused it. It was their fault. They did it to themselves. They were lost. It was too much. They weren't virgins. They were evil. Someone had to help them and that someone was me. Yeah, it was me, right? So, I'm not at fault, am I?'

'No, you're not. She and all the others were evil.'

'Yes, they were, stop it now.'

'Are you sure?'

'Yes, I'm sure. Everything will be fine.'

'Okay, I believe you. Thanks,' he said to himself, nodding at his reflection in the mirror.

EPISODE

12

The next week

Matthew was more than eager to start his new job, and like a lot of
people who start a new job, he would have to make new friends and he
wasn't the social type. Work was one thing but socializing outside of it
wasn't something he was interested in doing.

"Welcome, Matt," Kelly called out, loud enough for Rain to hear.

"Matt, it's great seeing you," Rain added.

"It's great seeing you guys as well. I told you I would be in your
department. Now I can keep my eyes on you," he smiled.

"Why does your cubicle have to be next to ours?"

"Connection, Rain!"

"Boy, you better stop before we get your ass fired on your first
day," Kelly said, as Rain and their co-workers laughed.

Just days after Matthew started working at Le Chic; he was
reprimanded for inappropriate behavior. Several of his female co-

workers complained that he was pushy in a sexual way. When confronted by Rain and Kelly, he denied it.

"It's all allegations, nothing more."

"Matt, you have to be careful," Rain warned him.

"All I did was ask them if they were married or had a boyfriend."

"What the fuck is wrong with you? Some of them know that you and I dated. You can't do that, come on now."

"She is right," Kelly added.

"Damn! It was only a question. I like women."

"We know you do, and this is why your dumb ass shouldn't have done what you did." Rain was pissed.

"But you know what, you're right."

"You're lucky they didn't fire your ass," she said.

"I promise I will behave."

"Don't promise me, do it for yourself." She walked away after warning him.

With a puzzled look on her face, Kelly asked, "What is wrong with that ex of yours? Who the fuck does that? He just started working here and already there are complaints against him."

"I really don't know what to say. I'm dumbfounded. I can't really put my finger on it, but he's been acting strangely for some time now. His obsession with women is getting scary, and it's rather troubling. Once when we were on the phone talking, he mentioned some freaky shit. Shit that he and I never did, and it bothered me."

"Are you serious?"

"No kidding, I ended the conversation real quick."

"I'm speechless. I don't know what to say."

"Girl, don't say another word. Let's see how things turn out."

***

That evening Rain and Jerry arranged to meet up at her favorite Chinese restaurant. After showering and getting dressed, her phone rang.

"Hey, Jordan!"

"Hey, did I call at a bad time?"

"Sort of."

"Okay, I'll call another time."

"I'm glad you understand, but I did appreciate the call, especially from my fellow writer."

Laughing, he responded, "I like that, but go ahead and we'll talk another time."

"Sure Jordan, bye."

***

She met with Jerry as planned, and as they ate, she brought up Matthew. She never mentioned they dated. Jerry listened as she spoke.

"Your co-worker sounds as if he has some issues."

"Issues? What do you mean?"

"Babes, he sounds like a perv."

"You think so?" she asked, trying not to laugh.

"Here it is you spoke on his behalf to your supervisors, and they hired him. Weeks later, there are a bunch of sexual complaints against him, and he thinks he's done nothing. Really?"

"I do agree that he's got some issues, but I don't think he's a pervert."

"I understand, he's your friend," he said, smiling as they changed the topic.

Rain was definitely not a picky eater, and Jerry made fun of her. They were going back and forth as they laughed and made fun of each other.

"Where does all that food go?" he asked. She couldn't help herself from bursting out in laughter.

"I am five-eleven what do you expect? I have to nourish my body. And if you want to know where all this food goes then you need to come and find out."

"Oh, no! No, you didn't! Okay. I'm going to find out." Laughing, she said, "Do you think you can climb this tree, as you put it?"

"Sure, I can, but I have to be honest, you're the tallest girl I've ever dated."

"Dated? Are we dating? I thought we . . ."

"Don't even go there," he laughed, cutting her off.

"I'll make a bet with you."

"What kind of bet?"

"If you can beat me in a game of one and one, I promise every Saturday for the next month, we'll do nothing but fuck the whole day."

"I'm gonna beat you, Rain."

"So, is it a bet?" she giggled.

"You bet!"

Rain was the best player on her high school basketball team and she and Kelly often played at the 14th Street recreation center. She made this known to Jerry and told him to show up with his "A" game, which he said he would. He constantly reminded her that he liked his women tall and that he would show her no mercy. To which she laughed and blew him a kiss.

"You are so competitive. I love that about you. I got you as I said."
He held her and smiled.

Rain wasn't in a hurry to go home. She wanted to stay with him a
bit longer, but he had to work the next day and so did she.

EPISODE

13

She got home sometime around eleven o'clock. And no sooner than she got settled, Kelly called. They were like two schoolgirls on the phone as they chatted. It was juvenile on their part, but it was fun.

"Oh, before I forget, Jerry wants to take me sailing."

"Sailing? Do you mean like the Circle Line? The Circle Line is for tourists."

"No girl, on his father's yacht. Weren't you listening to the things I have been telling you for the past months? His father is Wall Street millionaire, Herbert Benjamin."

"Oh shit, yeah, that's right. I almost forgot."

"Whatever!" Rain laughed. "I didn't know what to say when he asked."

"So, you're going?"

"Yes, and you're coming."

"Say what now?"

"I said, you're coming."

"I guess I have no choice, huh?"

"You don't," Rain said, teasing her. "Who would have thought that a guy I cursed out in a taxi would end up in a relationship with me and his father a multi-millionaire?"

"Me, because shit like this only happens in New York City."

"You're right, but do you think I should go?"

"Go? Girl, are you crazy? If you don't wanna go, then let me go, shoo!"

"But you were just saying . . ."

"My brain was in sleep mode — it's awake now," Kelly said, cutting her off, laughing.

Rain laughed as they continued talking. Kelly had a humorous side to her that was refreshing. She'll say things that will make you laugh even when you're being serious.

***

"What is it, Matt?" Rain asked him.

"I have tickets to the New York Aquarium, the Bronx Zoo, and some events in Central Park and I want to know if you would like to go with me."

"I don't know. I'm kind of busy."

"Rain, this is me. It's not like I'm your new boyfriend, you know, the rich guy," he laughed.

"You know what . . .?"

"Okay, I'm sorry. I was only joking."

She was reluctant about going, but the more they spoke the more she began taking a softer tone. The next day, the two met. They hugged. He complimented her on how she looked and immediately began behaving in a playful and alluring way.

As the day came to an end, they were exhausted and hungry. They walked to Rigoletto Pizza on the corner of 72nd Street. As they ate, Matthew made a conscious decision to find out where he stood with Rain. He had some remorse as he spoke.

"You know my love for you hasn't waned and it's difficult for me at times to even think." She was about to cut him off, but she let him continue. "I know at times I do some dumb things, but when I'm around you, I feel renewed. It pains me at times to see you with this new friend of yours. But I understand. Yet it doesn't ease the pain. I've never loved anyone the way I love you."

"Matt, I don't know what to say. I know you still care, and I care about you as well. But things are different now. What you and I had meant everything to me. But I have moved on, and you will always be a part of my life no matter who is there."

"For most of my life, I was considered eccentric, different from others until I met you. It was a tall order as far as I was concerned. You kept me grounded. You made me feel special. It is that special thing that I yearn for, and only you provided it, and can still provide it."

"Matt, I told you; you will always be a part of my life. It's not like I would never date you again. I would, but only when the time is right." He smiled. He had gotten the reassurance that he needed. And as their day ended, they embraced and kissed each other on the cheek.

EPISODE

14

Rain met with Jordan several days later. He invited her to his apartment, but she politely declined. He wasn't pleased with her response, but he respected it. She knew his reputation and he was aware of it, yet it didn't stop him from trying.

"Is this the complete manuscript?" he asked her as they sat in Starbucks.

"Yes, it is."

"From what I have read it sounds great. You can write your ass off. Here are the two books I promised."

"Oh wow, thanks, I almost forgot; here's mine," she smiled, handing it to him.

"Great! What are you doing two days from today?"

"I'm free, why?"

"I want you to meet someone special. She's an agent and I think you will like her. I think you two will get along fine. She lives in Northern New Jersey and she's having a party this weekend and I want you to come."

"Wow! That's cool. Can I bring, Kelly?" He hesitated before agreeing. He wanted Rain to himself and thought having Kelly there wouldn't work in his favor.

But what the hell, he thought to himself; *at least I'm making some progress.*

"It's right across the river, so you won't be too far."

"Where in Jersey is the party?"

"Exchange Place!"

"That's a nice neighborhood."

Exchange Place is a prestigious area with several high-rise buildings that rival New York City and offer a great panoramic view of the New York City skyline.

* * *

That night, Rain was in a reflective mood as she lay in bed. She considered herself a fun-loving person and wondered why she had taken the path in life she did, especially those spent with Jonathan.

But she was confident now and believed in herself. She wasn't the type to easily give up. A fighter, she questioned people and things that she didn't understand. A people person and a great friend, she would bend over backward or give her last if you needed it. Yet, she can be arrogant, overbearing, and difficult to deal with at times.

Being young, beautiful, educated, and female, shaped her in many ways. Growing up, she was told that she could achieve anything she wanted in life. Notwithstanding, she was a tomboy and she constantly heard that a pretty girl wasn't supposed to play rough and act tough. She was ridiculed by a lot of people who thought she shouldn't play basketball. Some thought she was gay. Others made comments such as "only gay girls play basketball." Initially, it bothered her, but then she thought *what about all those women who play professionally in the WNBA, Europe, and on playgrounds throughout the world? Are they all gay? No, they are not, and who are these people to tell me what sport I should play?*

As a young girl growing up in Toledo, she heard the stories of thugs taking over the streets and menacing the majority of low-income communities. She heard about the gang members who hung out on the street corners twenty-four hours a day. She remembered the stories she heard about gang members approaching underage girls, wanting to know if they were sexually active. Although she attended private school and was bused, she was friends with several girls from some of the poorer neighborhoods.

Some of these girls were young mothers and she saw the look of hopelessness and frustration in their eyes and on their faces. Seeing these things only reinforced the plans she had for herself, that is to make something of herself and get out of Toledo. She was well aware that attending private schools and living in an upscale community didn't shield her from some of the issues that affected her friends.

This had an impression on her, and it shaped her as she grew. She realized that some people are mean-spirited, ignorant, and misinformed. Realizing this, she knew she had to do things her way. She refused to let what others say define and shape her. Knowing the type of person that she is, her family and friends were shocked when she moved to Michigan with Jonathan and accepted his lifestyle. Yet she made a decision that was hers and she dealt with the consequences. She didn't want to become a statistic. She recognized that the relationship was heading in that direction, and she wanted out.

***

Several days later, Rain and Jerry met at the sports club for their one-on-one basketball game. It was intense as they both played hard, but the outcome favored, Jerry.

"You won the bet," she said to him out of breath.

"I know, and I'm gonna put it on you like a butcher put his knives to meat." They both laughed.

"What kind of saying is that?"

"It's a family thing," they continued laughing. "But you know what?"

"What?" she smiled with a naughty look on her face.

"You got game!"

"I told you. I've been playing since I was in middle school."

"Seriously babes, why didn't you try out for the WNBA?"

"I don't know. I guess I had a lot on my mind after college. Then I met Jonathan and I got distracted."

"Hmm, I see. You're just as good as some of those girls, if not better."

"Thanks," she smiled at him. "But you've got game too, babes."

"Game? I've got skills," he said, as they both laughed.

"Come on, let's go. We can shower at my place."

They discussed several issues as she drove to her apartment. Once there, they showered and made love.

"You had mentioned Jonathan at the gym, who is he?"

She realized that she had spoken too soon. She wasn't ready to discuss Jonathan and her marriage, but she had brought his name up, and knowing Jerry, he wanted to know more.

"My husband . . ."

"You are married?" he asked, sitting up in the bed.

"Startled," she murmured, "but, I'm in the process of getting a divorce."

"Oh, you are?"

"Yes."

She explained everything to him. He said he understood, but she should have told him; to which she apologized. He felt a considerable amount of empathy for her as she recalled the things Jonathan put her through. He was comforting throughout as she spoke. He felt relieved knowing she started the divorce process. Rain meant everything to him, and he told her so. He told her their encounter was destiny and that she was all that mattered to him.

That morning as he was getting dressed, she told him that she was invited to a party by a writer friend of hers. He kissed her goodbye and told her to give him a call.

"I will."

"Oh, are we still on for our cruise?"

"Of course, when do you want to do it?"

"How about next weekend? Is that good for you?"

"Yes." He closed the door behind him.

***

"Hi, Rain!"

"Hey, girl!"

"What are you doing tonight?"

"Tonight is Jordan's party."

"Oh, shit, I forgot about it."

"You've got issues, Kelly."

"I know, right!"

"Come on over and we'll leave together."

"Okay, I'll be there." Within minutes, Kelly arrived. "Is he supposed to meet us?" she asked as they were getting dressed.

"Shit, let me call him." He told her to meet him at Thirty-Fourth Street by the Macy's on the corner.

They met as planned and headed to the Holland Tunnel for the ten-minute drive into Jersey City. There they were introduced to several authors: Savannah J, Brooklen Borne, Dena Tyson, Dimples, and others in the publishing business. Rain was thrilled as she mingled and chatted with them. This is what she envisioned and to see it come to fruition was everything she hoped for. She assumed Jordan knew the authors, she and Kelly were introduced to, but that was not the case.

Jordan kept his word and spoke highly of her to Sandy Jenkins. She was impressed with the things that he shared. She gave Rain her card and told her they needed to talk and that she would love to see her work. Rain had a wonderful time and she thanked Jordan.

"The possibilities are endless for you, Rain. Sandy thinks highly of you, and she just met you," Jordan said to her as they drove back to the city.

"I really don't know what to say."

"I'll say it for you. You better go ahead and do what you need to do," Kelly said before either of them could say another word.

"Kelly is right," he went on, "take advantage of your situation because this business is not for the weak, but for those who are willing to take advantage of every opportunity that comes their way."

"You guys are right."

"Of course, we are," Kelly added.

"I can't believe I met all those wonderful authors."

"Get used to it, because as long as you're a part of my circle you will be meeting the movers and shakers in the business."

"Thanks a million, Jordan."

"It's okay," he smiled, staring at her gorgeous figure.

Back in the city, he dropped the ladies off in front of Kelly's apartment building. Although he had done a lot for Rain, she didn't want to disclose any information to him about where she lived, at least not yet. After sharing this with Kelly, she understood.

"I guess because he knows where I live, it's okay, huh?"

"Yeah! He's your friend. You introduced us." The two laughed aloud.

EPISODE

15

He spotted her running just after 8 p.m. on the East Side of Central Park. He followed her. Within minutes, she had made her way to the West Side of the park. She had her earphones on as she ran past the small reservoir listening to her music. It was dimly lit, but not dark enough for someone to take the chance and commit a crime. Although there was a police presence inside the park, and she knew there had been several murders in the surrounding neighborhood; she felt safe.

She saw a figure emerge from the dark and thought it was unusual. She was about to scream when the figure alighted from the bushes and knocked her to the ground, dragging her into the bushes. He punched her several times in the face. Dazed from the blows, he turned to see if anyone saw or heard anything, as he continued his brazen assault. As his helpless victim lay amongst the dirt, thorns, and bushes, he put a pair of latex gloves on and put his hands around her throat, strangling her.

He calmly removed her clothes, before peering through the bushes, making sure he had a clean getaway. Dressed in runner's attire, and with a nefarious frown, he coolly jogged away from the scene and blended in with the other runners.

Unstable, erratic, unafraid, and pragmatic at times, he hurriedly entered his apartment. After taking a shower, he ate and sat down in front of the mirror.

'How did I do tonight?'

'You did well.'

'I did?'

'Yes, you did.'

'But I didn't know if she was a whore.'

'Are you questioning me?'

'No, I'm not, but what if she wasn't?'

'Believe me, she was. Have I ever steered you wrong?'

'No, never!'

'There you go, trust me, she deserved it.'

'Yes, she did. You're right! And her hair was dark.'

'Good! We are not done.'

'We aren't?'

'No! Get dressed and find another one.'

'Now?'

'No, next year. Of course, I meant now!'

'Okay, I'm going, don't be mad at me.'

'I'm not. You are doing great. We'll talk when you get back.'

'Okay, I'm going.'

***

Not only was he bold, but his sole purpose was also to embarrass the police and make a mockery of the force. He wanted his next victim to be as close to the Central Park murder as possible. Was it a bluff? Quite the contrary! His next victim was a mere nine blocks from where the killing took place. No one thought he would be so daring.

He was already inside the building when she entered. He knocked her to the floor in the vestibule of the building and began punching her. He felt no remorse as he snatched her keys from her hand and dragged her onto the elevator. She was terrified as she stared at the masked man. Putting his hand over her mouth and warning her not to scream, they entered the apartment. He was in a twisted frenzy as he quickly tied her up, as she sobbed.

"Please, don't do this," she begged.

"I have to," he countered. She immediately realized what type of person she was dealing with.

"No, you don't have to. No one saw you. The camera doesn't work. The new ones won't be in place until next week."

"Is that so?"

"Yes. I won't say a word to anyone about this, not the police, no one."

"Hmm, I don't trust you."

"Yes, you can trust me."

"I can?"

"Yes, please let me go."

"But he told me not to."

"Who told you this?"

"Him."

"Him, who?"

"Him, never mind." Covering her mouth and putting a handkerchief soaked with chloroform over her nose, she slipped into unconsciousness within minutes. Using a piece of fishing line, he strangled her.

He removed her clothes and as she lay there, he stared at her lifeless body. He smiled admiring his work before fleeing. Back in his apartment, he took his usual shower and sat down in front of the mirror.

The next day, the city woke up to the shocking news. Two women were murdered only hours apart and nearby. The police were visibly upset as a city on the verge of hysteria lashed out at them. The tension was taking its toll. The women in the neighborhood feared for their lives.

The investigators assigned to the case weren't saying much to the public, except that they were sure that his removing the women's clothing had become his calling card. They were convinced that he removed their clothing once they were dead.

***

Things had taken a turn for the better for Matthew. The tension at the workplace had eased somewhat and he was now getting along great with his co-workers. One evening after work, Kelly invited him and Rain to her apartment. They were having drinks and discussing a range of topics when Matthew brought up the recent killings.

"Hey, you guys need to be careful because the police can't seem to arrest this guy. He's right under their nose and they keep overlooking him."

"I know, right? But how do you know he's right under their nose?" Kelly asked.

"Because they keep setting up all these checkpoints and have cops stationed everywhere and this mutha-fucka is still out there getting away with murder, literally."

"He is, and that I don't get, but I know they better make an arrest soon because people are getting scared," Rain added. "Shit, I'm scared!"

"Me too," Kelly went on.

"You gotta be careful. He attacked two women right here in this neighborhood. That's a bold son of a bitch. And if you notice all the women that were killed had dark hair."

"Matthew, we know that. But he's not gonna drive me away from this neighborhood. I've worked too damn hard to get into this building, and I'll be damned if I'm gonna let him scare me off."

"That's how you look at it? So, you think he can't get to you?"

"Matthew, what kind of bullshit is this? Why the fuck do you keep bringing up that shit?" Rain asked him, upset.

"Because I care about you two, that's why."

"Okay, but sometimes you say some crazy shit."

"Yeah, dude, you do," Kelly added.

"Fair enough, I won't say shit. I'll keep my mouth shut."

"Yes, you do that," both women responded.

Throughout the evening, Matthew kept nagging, Rain. He brought up their last conversation. It was immediately dismissed. He was more than determined as he again tried to make his case. She tried her best to be respectful, which at times was difficult. She repeatedly reminded him that she wasn't interested. The few drinks he had were affecting him. At times he was belligerent and frustrated. She knew how to get under his skin and before long; he was making his way out the door; without even a goodbye.

"What is wrong with that man? I keep telling you that something is wrong with him, and you keep saying no," Kelly remarked. "Everything was going great and then out of nowhere, he goes on a rant about the killings and then wants to get back with you."

"I don't know what to say. As I said in the past, he wasn't like this when we were together. I don't know what's gotten into him. Honestly, I get scared at times, and the shit that he says, I don't know. It's crazy, that's all I can say." Rain could only shake her head as she spoke. Both women had drunk way too much, and at Kelly's urging, Rain decided to spend the night.

EPISODE

16

That weekend

The evening was perfect, a soft breeze blew as the sunlight began to fade. Rain wore a black silk Dolce and Gabbana dress with black shoes, a Prada purse, and a pair of diamond earrings, as she waited in front of her apartment building. Seconds later, a black Maybach Mercedes Benz pulled to the curb beside her, behind the wheel was Jerry.

Talk about luxury, it caught the attention of several onlookers. It was fully loaded and worth every penny. He got out of the car and opened and held the passenger side door for her. Who said chivalry was dead? Rain was speechless as she smiled. It was quite the scene as he drove off. She was surprised — to see what he was wearing. Dressed in a tank top, khaki shorts, and sandals, she had a look of disappointment on her face, but he quickly reassured her that he was going to change.

"Wow! You are so beautiful. Gorgeous, babes! Simply gorgeous," he stated, smiling.

"Thank you. I thought I overdid it when I saw you."

"You mean the way I'm dressed?"

"Yes."

"Don't worry about it. As I said, I'm going to change," he winked at her, smiling.

"Is everything okay?" he asked, seeing the look on her face.

"Yes, just a bit unnerved."

"And why is that?"

"I don't know. Maybe it's because Kelly couldn't make it."

"I was expecting her as well. But you told me she had some family issues, right?"

"Yeah. You're right. I was just worried that's all. Maybe it's the way how things are going."

"Babes, I think you're putting too much pressure on yourself."

"Maybe it's just me."

"We don't have to do this. We can do something else."

"Oh, no."

"Are you sure?" he smiled.

"Yes," she replied in her cutest little girl voice.

"I get it. Your best friend and the things that concern you matter. I completely understand."

"Thanks for understanding."

"This is what I do, babes," he said, smiling.

He headed towards the Williamsburg Bridge and caught the Brooklyn Queens Expressway, where he later merged onto the Long Island Expressway. Within minutes, they were in the Hamptons. He pulled up to the pier and a young man greeted them and addressed Jerry as if he was a celebrity. Rain was very observant as the young man got behind the wheels and parked it several yards away.

"That's her, right there!" Jerry pointed.

"Who?" Rain asked, before realizing he was talking about his yacht.

Her exterior and part of the interior were painted white. The deck was painted a gleaming jet-black color. She was not only beautiful. She was immaculate. Rain's heart was pounding as he led her aboard.

"Wait here!" he said, disappearing from her view.

When he finally appeared, he was wearing a gray linen Armani shirt and black shorts with gray Brunomagli sandals. *He looked sexy*, she thought — as he motioned for her to sit down.

"Is this better?"

"Yes, it is," she giggled.

"Now I need you to do the same, go ahead. There's a change of clothes there."

"Change? You want me to change? I didn't bring a change of clothes," she remarked.

"I know, but I did. I got you," he said, smiling. She laughed, walking away. She returned wearing a wrap skirt, matching top, and a pair of leather thong sandals.

He took two bottles of Krug champagne from a small refrigerator. He handed her two glasses and a bowl of potato chips. They looked at each other and began laughing.

"This is just for starters," he said, trying to contain his laughter.

"Are you sure?"

"I don't know. We might wind up having some Cheez-Doodles next."

"This is too much," Rain chuckled, wiping her eyes.

He put the yacht on automatic pilot as they drank and ate potato chips. Rain was having the time of her life as they slowly sailed away from the pier. They kissed and flirted with each other. The view was spectacular as the huge mansions became smaller as the yacht sailed into deeper waters. The water gave off an unthreatening boom as it gently crashed against the yacht. There were several yachts out at sea; some were blasting loud music as their occupants partied.

Jerry anchored his yacht in a quiet area in the Sound. Rain was getting turned on as he held her in his arms and stared into her eyes. He kissed her on the neck as his fingers searched gently under her top, finding and rubbing her breasts. She pressed her erect nipples against his manly chest and reached for his manhood. She opened his zipper and began jerking it back and forth. He pulled up her skirt and began playing with her moist garden of love.

To her amazement, he dropped to his knees stuck his head under her skirt, and began kissing her wet garden. He pulled her panties to the side and slowly and deliberately began running his tongue in and around her swollen lips. It feels good, she sighs, in a low whisper. She held onto the rail and with all her strength, she slowly began gyrating her swollen secret garden over his tongue and face. She thought he was going to fuck her as he turned her around. Instead, he kissed and licked her ass cheeks and ran his tongue between them. She was going out of her mind as the cool summer breeze hit her ass.

She felt like one of the characters in her book as she loosened his shorts and pulled them down. His erect manhood stood at attention. She teasingly caressed it. He was going out of his mind. He was ready to explode when he bent her over against the cabin door and entered her. She met his every thrust as they yelled, screamed, and moaned without fear of anyone hearing them. He held her by the hips as his intensity built. His thrusts were quick and powerful, and Rain met his every stroke as they raced to a climax. Sweating profusely and with his legs trembling, he exploded deep inside her. They cleaned themselves up and sailed back to the pier. Thinking the date was over; she was surprised to find out he made plans for them to have dinner on the pier.

They had grilled Cornish hen and steamed shrimp in garlic sauce with steamed vegetables. To top it off, they had two four-hundred-dollar bottles of Blanc De Noir champagne. It didn't take long for the champagne to take effect. It was romantic as they sat under the stars eating and listening to the waves as they calmly rolled ashore.

"I want to show you something," he said after their meal.

They walked to the end of the pier where he pointed toward the New York skyline, it was breathtaking. Nothing compared to the view from the Hamptons. Rain didn't want the night to end as Jerry held her around her waist. She felt his throbbing member rubbing against her. His hands caressed her body. He moved them upward and gently squeezed her breast. She held his hands against them and shoved her ass on his dick. He slid his hands down to her love nest and began groping her threshold. She was aroused as she played with her tits.

"Let's go on the yacht," he whispered in her ears. She was so far gone; that she didn't say a word. They ended the night with a well-deserved nightcap.

EPISODE

17

Rain filled Kelly in on her date with Jerry; telling her they had a blast. Kelly was supportive and happy for her, despite her family worries, most of which, she said, were working themselves out. Rain understood, telling her she had her full support. As their conversation continued, Rain brought up, Jordan. Kelly wasn't as forthcoming as she had been when she first heard about Jerry.

Rain visited Jordan twice at his place of business and for some unknown reason; Kelly told her it wasn't a good idea. When she insisted on knowing why — Kelly began explaining.

"He's a player and I'm quite sure you know this. I just don't want you to get involved in his world. It's about money, women, and pussy as far as he's concerned. He has no respect for women. He thinks they are only good for one thing and that's fucking."

"Okay, I know what he's up to, but my thing is to get my other books published and build up a favorable network with some of the people he introduced me to."

"That's cool, but don't let him convince you to go to his apartment. Didn't he ask you?"

"He sure did, but it didn't happen then and it's not ever going to happen. Jerry is who I belong to." They burst out in laughter.

"He's got you like that, Rain?"

Giggling, she said, "I think so."

"You guys seem serious, and this is why I was telling you not to get caught up in that fool and his games."

"As I said, you don't have to worry about that ever happening."

"Oh, before I forget, what's going on with the divorce?"

"I did what I was supposed to do, and now I'm waiting, that's it."

"You think he'll sign it?"

"What's the sense in him not signing it?"

"You know how some men are, but then again, he should want to, as you said. I hope he does so you can get on with your life."

"I feel confident that he will." The women spoke at length before heading home.

Kelly didn't get into all the details with Rain; however, she knew she and Jordan met on several occasions. According to Kelly, she was saying one thing and doing another. Since their conversation, Rain reassured her that wasn't the case. Rain was pissed at her and she made it known. Kelly would show her displeasure whenever Rain would invite her to party with her and Jordan.

***

It had been a while since Rain spoke to Tatyana about her and Jerry's ongoing relationship. And it wasn't long before she called and updated her with the latest details. Tatyana wasn't aware that she and Matthew were no longer a couple. She knew about their off-and-on relationship and if anything, she thought they would eventually get back together. In her mind, Jerry was sort of an afterthought. Even so, she was happy for Rain.

"Maybe, you'll be the first to get married again," Tatyana said to her.

Laughing, she replied, "Marriage? Again? That soon? You've got me married already, huh?"

"Hey, you never know. This might be the start of something. You know what I'm saying?"

"Girl, you're way ahead of the game. So, what's going on with you?"

"Wait. I'm not done yet. What's going on with you and Kelly?"

"She's pissed at me for hanging out with that author I was telling you about."

"Y'all need to stop that bullshit. It's not that serious."

"He is her friend. I met him through her."

"You guys need to chill with that."

"It's not me. It's her."

"She called me a few days ago and was complaining about me not partying with y'all like I used to. I told her that I've been busy and as soon as I visit, we can all go and hang out."

"That's a good idea. You need to bring your ass to the city."

"I know, right? But I'm gonna put it on my itinerary."

"Your what? You've got to be kidding."

"No, I'm not," she said, laughing. "I've got a busy life, big sis."

Laughing, Rain said, "I'm gonna beat your ass when I see you."

"No, you won't. You've got a man to occupy your time now. But seriously, I hope you and Kelly work that out."

"We will. She'll get over it."

"Yeah, she will. What's going on with the divorce?"

"I'm waiting. I did everything that I was supposed to do. He'll sign it, trust me."

"Just keep me posted."

"I will. Anyways, how is grandma?"

"She's not doing so well. The medication the doctors gave her has been giving her some terrible side effects."

"What kind of side effects?"

"Abdominal pain."

"I need to give her a call."

"I think you should. I heard from mother."

"Oh, you did?" Rain asked, not in the least concerned.

"Yeah, I overheard her and grandma arguing about some guy."

"But why would grandma argue with her about her love life? She's a grown-ass woman. What were they saying?"

"Grandma was saying that she needs to settle down at her age and stop trying to be 'your daughter's age.' I wanted to laugh but I didn't want them to know I was listening. Mother was screaming at her. She told grandma to stay out of her life because she didn't know what she was talking about. But grandma would have none of it; she told her she had enough money to last a lifetime, and that she needed to realize that life isn't some kind of party. And that she was getting old. I was laughing my ass off."

"She's right. Mother needs to stop her Tina Turner routine," Rain added.

"Mother says she's in love and she could care less what grandma, or you and I think."

"How did we get in that shit? I hope she doesn't bring any of that bullshit to me."

"Tell me about it, but that's what she said. I couldn't take anymore so I interrupted them and told them I was leaving."

"Good for you!" they both laughed.

"All I know is it's an on-and-off relationship."

"Okay. I'm going to give her and grandma a call."

"Good luck," Tatyana said.

"Oh, I almost forgot, Jerry and his family are having a party and I want you to come."

"When is it?"

"No date as yet, but I'll let you know."

"Okay!"

"I just have to convince Kelly to show up, and that's it."

"She'll be there. You guys will work it out."

"Okay! Bye!"

After their conversation, Rain was in a reflective mood. She hadn't thought much about the progress she and Jerry had made in such a short period. She was having a wonderful time, but she had broken one of her rules, and that was never to give it up until at least the fourth try. She came close. But close wasn't good enough, at least that's what she thought, she gave it up on the second attempt. She was smitten and would have probably given it up on their first date.

What she couldn't get over was the fact that she had performed oral sex on him on their second date and he had his way with her. But she was convinced that he was smitten as well, and he was. She wondered if he had thought she was easy and a freak. *Did he see me in a different light? Maybe he thought I acted too damn uppity that night in the cab and look how quickly we fucked after that. I fucked up!* she thought to herself.

EPISODE

18

To avoid the stress, she was putting herself through, Rain decided to do some writing. So much was happening and at times it seemed surreal as she tried to multi-task and make sense of it all. Getting an agent as Jordan suggested, was a great idea. Her agent had accepted Jordan's offer for the two to do a book signing together. Eager for the exposure, it was a no-brainer, and she agreed. As her fingers stroked the keyboard, she thought about the recent chain of events that had changed her life. Lost in her thoughts, it took her several seconds before she realized that her phone was ringing. It was her mother and she sounded annoyed and agitated. She tried her best to calm her down.

"Mother, what's the matter?"

"Je suis en colère!" (It means I'm mad.)

"Why and at who?"

"It's your grandmother; you need to tell her to stop calling your sister and telling her my business."

Laughing, she said, "You mean like you did with me and Tatyana?" She couldn't help herself as she too began to laugh.

"Okay, you're right, but this woman wants me to act like I'm fifty years old."

"But mother, you are fifty."

"Correction darling, I'm a young fifty. I'm full of life, soothing with love, and exuberant in all aspects of my lifestyle." She was right; she lived her life like Valarie Pettiford the actress who played the larger-than-life bourgeoisie mother on the television series Half & Half.

"Mother, why don't you talk with her?"

"You mean when hell freezes over? Your grandmother complains that I cozy up with too many young men. I think she wants me to befriend older guys. I told her to look after Fifi for me this weekend because I'll be spending the weekend in St. Tropez with my new boyfriend at his villa in La Croix Valmer. You know darling, the weather there is marvelous. You should find yourself a nice young man yourself and enjoy life."

"Mother, you can leave Fifi with me, it's not a problem."

"It's okay, honey, she insisted on keeping her."

"I see."

"Rain!"

"Yes."

"Did that no good soon-to-be ex-husband of yours sign the divorce papers?"

"I'm assuming he did. I think he did. I'm waiting."

"Well, I hope he did. So, you can move on with your life."

"Mother, I have moved on."

"You know what I mean, and your sister told me about your new friend. Whatever happened to Matthew? Where is he? And what is he doing now?"

"Oh, she mentioned him? Her and her big mouth! If you must know, I got him a job at Le Chic."

"Oh, that was certainly nice, but what made . . ."

"He's a nice guy despite our rocky relationship," she said, cutting her mother off.

"That's an understatement if I ever heard one. He's a stalker and a . . ."

"Mother, enough! Thank you!"

"Dear, dear, I'm sorry. Well, it's time to feed, Fifi. Did you know that I bought her a gold bowl to eat from?"

"Mother, grr!"

"Okay, I'm going to feed her. Love you and take care of yourself. Oh, how is the book thing coming along?"

"Great! I will discuss it with you next time. I love you mother and please sit down and talk to grandma."

"Okay sweetie, bonne nuit!"

"Bonne nuit, mother."

***

Rain and Kelly decided to clear the air. Their friendship meant everything. Jordan, sensing something was off, downplayed the interaction between him and Rain as one of those things. He thought nothing of her behavior. He summed it up as nothing more than she and her boyfriend having problems. He hadn't met Jerry, but he knew she was seeing someone. Yet it never stopped him from flirting and asking her out on a date. That same week, Tatyana showed up. The women readied themselves that weekend for Jerry's private party.

It was lights, camera, and action, as the three women elegantly entered and greeted the crowd. Jerry was more than excited as he greeted the three.

"Jerry, this is my sister, Tatyana," Rain said, introducing her.

"Hi, how are you?"

"I'm fine. I have heard a lot of wonderful things about you."

"That's great," he said, "I guess I'm a wonderful guy," he smiled, turning to look at Rain.

"She did say that."

"Great," he said, smiling. "And how are you doing, Kelly?" She smiled.

Taking Rain by the hand, he told her there was someone he wanted her to meet. She knew it was his parents. She was suddenly nervous. Sensing her discomfort, he told her not to worry, as Kelly and Tatyana followed closely behind.

"Mother, this is Rain," he said, approaching an elderly but beautiful woman. She spoke eloquently and said her name was Ruth.

"Hi, how are you?" Rain asked, extending her hand. Just then his father gently cleared his throat and smiled at him.

"This is father . . ."

"Herbert," he smiled, reaching for her hand. "You are as beautiful as my son described you." Rain blushed.

"Thank you."

"And who are these two beautiful women?" he continued.

"I'm Tatyana and I'm Kelly," they both replied.

The three women were nervous as Ruth introduced them to her socialite friends. They were amazed as they stared at the dazzling jewelry the women wore.

"Excuse me," Jerry said, interrupting the women, and taking Rain aside. "You look so yummy . . . I mean gorgeous," he smiled, taking her to another section of the mansion.

"Thanks, and you look your usual handsome self."

"Did you expect anything less?" they burst out in laughter. "I need to ask you something, but I don't want you to get upset. Is that okay with you?"

She was somewhat unsettled before saying, "Go ahead."

"How is the writing coming along?"

"It's coming along fine. But are you sure this is what you want to ask me?"

"Sure, I'm sure. How are things going with you and Jordan?"

"What do you mean?"

"Is he trying to push up on you?"

"Why would you ask me that?"

"Because I'm aware of him and his reputation."

"You never told me that you know him."

"I don't. I have friends who know him, and I have seen him on a few occasions at a few parties. A buddy of mine told me, he wanted to come tonight. But he told him it was an invite-only."

"I see. Well, you don't have to worry about him pushing up on me because it will never happen."

"And why is that?" he asked with a coy look on his face.

"Because I would never disrespect you like that."

"I understand. But it's not you, it's more about him."

"What do you mean?"

"Like a beatdown, you know what I mean?"

"No, Jerry. That is not necessary. As I said, never! I would never disrespect you or myself."

"I got you."

Breaking into a song, she began singing, "Hey, I've got you, baby. I've got you, baby." He couldn't help but join her.

"Really? You went Sonny and Cher on me?" he laughed.

"You joined me, didn't you?"

"Sure, you're right," he said, holding her around the waist. "Come, let's go and join the others."

They had a smashing time and so did Kelly and Tatyana. They drank and danced with Jerry, his father, and his mother. It was quite the scene as Ruth and Herbert who are divorced were together for most of the night. Their friendship was genuine, and Jerry was pleased that they had become such good friends. As the party ended, Rain gave her apartment and car keys to Tatyana. Smiling, she waved goodnight at her and Kelly. But instead of spending the night there, Tatyana stayed at Kelly's apartment.

***

"Since you've been here, you haven't said much," Kelly said to Tatyana.

"Yes, I have. Maybe I haven't said what you'd like me to say, is that it?"

"Don't patronize me."

"Patronize you? You were the one who stopped calling it wasn't me."

"The only reason I stopped was that I didn't want your sister to know about us."

"Are you kidding me?"

"So, are you saying she knows?" Kelly wasn't being truthful.

"No, I'm not saying that, but I'm quite sure my sister could care less about anything that's going on between me and you. So don't even go there."

"Look, that's the only reason why I stopped calling. It had nothing to do with anything else."

"So why didn't you say this when we last spoke?"

"I don't know. I guess I wasn't thinking."

"You are much older than me and yet I wonder at times."

"Wonder about what?"

"Whether you've got it all together."

"You mean like crazy?"

"Yeah," they laughed aloud.

"I can't believe you said that about me. That's fucked up!"

Laughing, she said, "No it's not!"

"I'm gonna fuck you up. You're sleeping on the couch, no that's too good for you. You're going on the floor."

"I'm sorry," she said, as they continued laughing.

Tatyana had a naughty look on her face as she grabbed Kelly around the waist and walked to the bedroom. Turning off the lights, they cuddle as the hours pass.

EPISODE

19

Across town

She was walking west towards W. 67th Street and Central Park West when he approached the soft-talking dark-haired woman. She had only moments ago walked with friends to the train station and was on her way back to her apartment.

"Nice night. Isn't it?" he said to her.

She looked at him and hurriedly crossed the intersection. Turning to see if he was still there, she was relieved when she didn't. As she walked past the slightly darkened passageway, he attacked her. Covering her mouth and threatening her at the same time, he took whatever identification she had.

Putting on a ski mask and gloves, he blended in perfectly with the few people who were out facing the blowing wind and cold. As the wind whipped across his face, he pulled the hoodie that he wore over his head and warned her, "You're going to take me to your apartment and you're not going to do anything stupid. You are going to act normal and if you do otherwise, you will die. Do you hear me?" he said in a calm but authoritative voice.

Trembling with fear, she uttered, "Okay."

They entered the building and got in the elevator. Seconds later, they were inside the apartment. Terrified and wanting to know why he attacked her, she begged him not to hurt her. He had a disturbed look on his face as he calmly brushed his cheek against hers and said, "I won't." He then tied her up and gagged her mouth. "Everything I say to you from this moment on, I want you to either nod yes or shake your head no. Do you hear me?" she nodded in agreement.

After asking her countless questions, he seemed satisfied with her response only to ask if she had a boyfriend and if she partied. She said yes, he reached inside his coat pocket and pulled out a bottle of chloroform. He removed the gag from her mouth, again warning her to remain quiet.

"Thank you," she said.

"Didn't I tell you to be quiet . . .? You're welcome, no I mean, sure . . ." He had a look of innocence on his face as his face twinged, unsure of what else to say.

"You know you're a handsome young man."

"I am?"

"Yes, you are," she answered, petrified.

"I've been told that before, but you think so?"

Without waiting for a response, he said aloud, 'Why are you mad at me? She only said that I'm handsome. Okay, I won't listen to her. I know I'm here to do a job. Okay, okay, I'm gonna do it.'

"What is it?" she repeated, trembling with fear.

He ignored her and instead pressed the chloroform hankie against her face, rendering her unconscious. He untied her and removed her clothing. He laid her on the floor and without any remorse he strangled her.

'Are you satisfied?!! Are you? You know it takes several minutes before the chloroform works, but you insist on me taking these chances,' he said under his breath. Nodding his head he answered, *'Yes, I am.'* He stared at her lifeless body before cleaning up and coolly leaving the apartment.

EPISODE

20

The three women had a wonderful time together that weekend. It was like old times. As for the sisters, they had some catching up to do, before Tatyana headed back to Massachusetts.

"Guess who I heard from?"

"Who?" Tatyana asked.

"Ashley Simmons."

"Really! I haven't seen her for such a long time. How is she doing?"

"She's thinking about coming to the city. I told her she can stay with me whenever she gets here."

"That's good; I would love to see her."

"I'll let you know when she gets here."

"Okay, that'll be nice."

"So, what do you think?"

"He's a nice guy. I'm impressed sis, and it seems like he's smitten."

"You think he is?" She was sure that he was, but she needed validation.

"Sis, anybody can see that you two are into each other."

"For real?" she smiled.

"Yes!"

"So, how are things with you and Kelly?"

"Huh?" she said, surprised. "What do you mean?"

"You think I don't know?"

"About?"

"You and Kelly!"

She had a slight smile on her face. "You knew?"

"Yes. You're my sister. I knew from the moment I first introduced you guys. I just didn't say anything."

"Oh, my God, sis! I didn't think you knew."

"I did. I was waiting for you to tell me."

"I was, but I figured you knew," they burst out in laughter.

"You're such a lying ass. So that's why you never told me?" she said, still laughing.

"Something like that; but we are okay now."

"Well, I'm glad because with everything that was going on; she was getting on my last nerve." They laughed aloud once again.

"She's fine now."

"That's good."

"You don't have to take me to the airport, she will."

"Okay, great. Now I can spend some time with my man on the phone and get some writing done."

Minutes later, Tatyana's phone rang, it was Kelly. The two sisters hugged and kissed each other bye. Tatyana then left for the airport.

***

Rain and Jerry were having lunch on the Upper Westside when Matthew appeared. Taken aback, there was some discomfort on Rain's part as he reached for Jerry's hand to shake it.

"Hi Matt, what are you doing on this side of town?"

"I was at the gym a few blocks from here working out."

"I see, but you're not dressed . . . Oh, I get it. You changed in the gym."

"I did babes . . . I mean, Rain."

"What the fuck you said, bro?" Jerry snapped.

"I'm sorry. I apologize."

Jerry was about to knock his ass out when Rain taps his legs under the table.

"But isn't it a coincidence that you saw us in this particular restaurant?" Rain said, doing her best to ease the tension.

"I was walking by, and something said to turn and look, and there you were. I guess it was a bit more than a coincidence. My horoscope said that I would encounter an ex-girlfriend," he smiled. He was being slick, and Jerry was only seconds away from beating his ass.

"Oh, I see," Rain responded tapping Jerry's legs once again. "Well, it was nice seeing you, Matt. See you at work."

"Will do, have fun. Nice seeing you again . . . Jerry, right?"

"Right, that's right," Jerry said, staring him down.

After he left, Rain told Jerry that she was baffled by his intrusion and behavior. "It's the second or third time that he has shown up unannounced," she continued.

"I was gonna kick his fucking ass!" Jerry snapped. "What the fuck was up with the baby talk?"

"I don't know where it came from, but I don't like it."

"And you say this is the second or third time this guy has popped up unannounced?"

"Yes, and I don't like it."

"This guy has some serious issues and he's going to be a problem."

"I think so too, but I'm going to straighten his ass out at work. It's beginning to look scary."

"Did he display any of these signs when you guys were dating?"

"No, he didn't. It was only after our breakup that I began noticing it."

"Well, if he ever shows up uninvited when you and I are together again, I'm gonna kick his ass that much I'll promise!"

"Baby, I'll deal with him."

"Yeah, you do that. I know expectation and delivering are two different things, but trust me on this, I will deliver if he shows up."

"Baby, it's not necessary, I'll take care of it."

That Monday

"Excuse me, Matt," Rain called to him as they headed to lunch.

"How can I help you, babes?"

"First of all, stop calling me babes! How dare you show up at the restaurant? What the fuck is your problem? And why the fuck are you stalking me? Are you some kind of a stalker?"

"What are you talking about?"

"Your showing up was rude and uncalled for. I was with my man. How dare you? Stay the fuck away from me, Matt. I mean it; stay the fuck away from me."

"So, you're saying that if I had shown up like the other times when you were by yourself, it would have been cool?"

"What the fuck don't you get, huh?"

"I'm sorry for showing up, but it was a mere coincidence."

"Your timing was no mere coincidence. You know what? I don't care what it was at this moment. Do me a favor and stay the fuck away from me. Do you hear me?"

"Okay, if that's what you want, fine!" he said, angrily walking away.

"Yes, that's what I want!" she said, loud enough for him to hear.

Kelly, who was looking for Rain, was surprised upon hearing the last exchange between the two, as they went their separate ways.

"What happened?" Kelly asked.

"Matt, he keeps showing up uninvited like a damn stalker. He showed up while Jerry and I were having lunch."

"What the fuck! How disrespectful!"

"That's the same thing I said."

"I told you he's changed. He's not the same."

"I'm seeing it now and I don't like it. Jerry said if he shows up again, he's going to beat his ass."

"Maybe that's what he needs."

"All I know is that I told him not to fuck with me anymore."

"You mean it?"

"Yeah, at least until he gets his shit together and starts acting like he's still got some damn sense."

"I understand. He's lucky Jerry didn't knock his ass out. That's a diesel-looking brother." They laughed.

The two ended their conversation and went back to work. The stand-off between Rain and Matthew went on for weeks without them speaking to each other.

EPISODE

21

Rain was prepared as she gathered the books for her book signing with Jordan. She felt optimistic because it was only days earlier her publisher had received her manuscript. She gathered her belongings and drove to Kelly's apartment, where she waited for Jordan's call.

"I'll meet you downstairs," she said to Jordan.

"Downstairs at your place?" he asked.

"No, I'm at Kelly's place."

"Oh!" he said, sounding a bit surprised. "I'll be there in five." He hung up the phone.

"I sure wish you could come," Rain said to Kelly, who had promised to visit her mother.

"You know I would have if I hadn't promised my mom."

"I know. I'm kinda nervous."

"You'll be fine. This is what you have been waiting for your whole life. I know what I said earlier you didn't take kindly to, but I know you'll take care of yourself."

"Thanks. I feel a whole lot better." They hugged each other as Rain made her way downstairs.

"You look gorgeous," a beaming Jordan smiled, putting her belongings in the back of his SUV.

"Thank you," she replied.

"So, are you ready to make some money and network at the same time?"

"I guess."

"What do you mean you guess?"

"I'm so nervous."

"You will be fine, don't worry about it."

"If you say so; you mentioned something about networking."

"Yeah, it's an indoor book show, signing, and expo."

"Oh, wow! So, a lot of people are gonna be there?"

"Yup, but you'll be fine. Hey, let me ask you something."

"Sure."

"I'm starting to get the impression that you don't want me to know where you live. What's that all about?"

"Jordan not now, and it's not that either."

"So, what is it then?"

"It's my boyfriend."

"Oh okay, so because of him you don't want me to know?"

"Jordan, not now!"

"Okay, you got it." Within minutes, they arrived at the Jacob Javits Convention Center.

Located on the Westside of Manhattan, the expo is a yearly event and unlike other exhibitions; it's one of the most recognized and important literary showcases for publishers, editors, comic book writers, motivational speakers, seasoned and new authors, and readers alike. It attracts people from all over the world. It's not unusual to meet and greet celebrities and some of the literary world's most noted speakers and established authors. The event is also broadcast around the world.

Jordan had paid the required fee. Their table was on the main floor. There were several booths and tables strewn throughout. The two eagerly sat down and welcomed the day's event with open arms. Rain was overcome by the jitters and seeing this, Jordan did his best to calm her. He assured her that once she made her first sale, she would be fine. It wasn't long before she was relaxed and networking with her peers and others. Seeing her publishing company there, helped her tremendously as her confidence got a needed boost. The two sold all their books. It was an event that was well worth it, Rain would later say.

Rain was worried about Kelly not being home as they drove to her apartment. She texted her earlier but did not get a response. They were minutes away from her apartment when her phone rang. There was a look of relief on her face as she answered. Jordan didn't say much as they drove. He was still upset at her because she still hadn't told him where she lived. As the SUV came to a stop in front of Kelly's apartment building, she noticed Matthew as he stepped from between two parked cars. There was an expressionless look on his face as their eyes met. He coolly waved and stared at Jordan. Jordan was unnerved; and when Matthew suddenly stopped, he asked Rain if she knew who he was.

"Yes, I know him," she replied.

"He knows Kelly, too?"

"Yeah, he works with us. I know what you're thinking . . ."

"Isn't that your car he's standing next to?" he said, cutting her off.

"Yeah, it is."

"That's a creepy guy . . . but what were you saying?"

"He's my ex."

"Your ex?! So, what is he doing around here?"

"I don't know. I'm as baffled as you are. Don't worry about him."

"Okay, do you need me to walk you inside?"

"Thanks, but I'll be fine. Aren't you coming upstairs?"

"No, I have a few stops to make. Spend the money you made wisely," he smiled at her.

"I will," she giggled.

As Jordan drove off, Matthew stared at him from the opposite side of the street. *Hmm, he said to himself.* He rolled his window down and was about to say something, but quickly changed his mind. He glanced in his rearview mirror, but to his surprise, Matthew had disappeared.

Meanwhile upstairs

"I can't believe you sold that many books," a jubilant Kelly said to Rain.

"Me too, it was supposed to be a networking event and it was for the most part; but Jordan knew what he was doing."

"That's great. But what was all that you were saying about him still wanting to know where you live?"

"He's insistent on wanting to know where I live. He just doesn't get it."

"I think because he introduced you to some of the people in the industry, he feels you owe him."

"If he does that's his problem, not mine. But I hear you. You know I never asked you how long you guys have known each other."

"Long enough!"

"Oh, that's a long time."

"It is, right?"

"Guess who we saw when we pulled up?"

"You know I'm not good at guessing. Who was it?"

"Matthew."

"Matthew? What the fuck was he doing around here?"

"I don't know. I thought he was here."

"No, I visited my mom and came back here. I didn't see him when I got back."

"Maybe he knows somebody around here."

"Maybe. He probably was visiting one of his bitches." The women laughed.

"I'm not gonna say anything to him about this."

"He saw you?"

"Yeah, he stared at me and Jordan."

"I don't like the sound of this. I'm gonna say something when I go back to work."

"Yeah, you do that. I need a drink. Whatcha got to drink?"

"A little bit of this, a little bit of that. Oh, I have some Hennessy pure white, want some?"

"Yeah, let me have some." As she did so, she called Jerry, in case she needed a ride. She was disturbed by Matthew and Jordan's behavior and feared anyone of them could follow her home. So, leaving her car behind made sense.

EPISODE

22

It was a shock to Kelly as she approached Matthew's cubicle, he and Rain were in a heated conversation. Although they weren't loud, anyone walking by could hear. It seemed Rain had changed her mind. She was furious.

"This has to stop, Matt! What is your problem?" she asked him, as Kelly joined them.

"I told you I was in the neighborhood taking care of some business."

"You're always taking care of business in the same part of town as me? You think I'm fucking stupid?"

Turning to Kelly, he said, "I was going to stop by your place. She would have never seen me if I had just left, but no, I thought about my friend. I was walking to your building when my phone rang. It was an important call, and so I decided to turn around and that's when I saw her," he argued.

"Matt, it doesn't look good. I hear your point and I would have loved it if you had stopped by, but it's bothering her, can't you understand that?"

"Kelly, it's just a coincidence," he pleaded.

"Coincidence my ass," Rain snapped.

"What's with the condescending tone and attitude, Rain? It's me, Matt!"

"Don't patronize me!"

"Patronize you? See, this is what I'm talking about . . ."

"Guys, enough! People are starting to look," Kelly warned them.

"Stay away from me, Matt."

"You're crazy!"

"Matt!" a frustrated Kelly yelled, as their co-workers turned to look.

"Okay! I'm done." Kelly put her arm around Rain's shoulder and the two walked back to her cubicle.

"I don't know what else to do. I have had it up to here."

"Don't let him get the best of you."

"But he keeps showing up every fucking where I turn. I'm sick of that shit, and I don't wanna have to go to the police."

"The police won't help. He hasn't done anything, and can you prove that he's stalking you? That's the shit they're gonna ask."

"I'm so damn fed up."

"Don't worry, it will be alright."

***

Jerry was bothered by Matthew's behavior. He couldn't understand why he would continue showing up unannounced. He thought about paying him a personal visit, but he knew Rain would get upset. The two were discussing other matters over lunch when Rain brought him up. Needless to say, Jerry didn't want to discuss it.

"The guy is a stalker."

"It's beyond that babes, he's starting to give me the creeps."

"I said it before and I'll say it again, why did you get him a job at your workplace?"

"Don't go there, Jerry! Not now, please."

"I'm sorry." After finishing their lunch, they drove to Jerry's apartment where they spent the rest of the day.

***

Wind and rain interrupted the quiet night. Not a soul was on the street — except for a few speeding cars. Across the street from Matthew's apartment, an idled car with its engine running and three men inside waited. Minutes later, an unsuspecting Matthew walked out of the building ran to his car, and drove off. The car with the three men followed closely behind. Moments later, Matthew pulled up in front of an apartment building. He got out of the car and began walking towards the building — drenched from the rain when he was confronted by the three men. Fearing for his life, he tried to make a run for it, only to be met with a crushing blow to the side of his head.

"What the fuck is this?" he cried out.

"Shut the fuck up!" one of the men balked at him. "Bring his ass to the car." They did.

They drove him to a secluded area and beat him senseless. Somehow, he made his way to a well-lit area and called for help. Minutes later, he was taken by ambulance to the hospital. He had several broken ribs, a broken nose, and numerous lacerations. When news of this got back to Rain and Kelly they were upset. Rain certainly didn't wish him any harm.

"Who could have done this to him?" Kelly asked.

"I have no idea," Rain replied.

"Did you have anything to do with it?"

"No, why would I? He was a thorn in my side but, I wouldn't do that to him. And who do I know that would do it?"

"Jerry! He's got money and connection and it's not like he doesn't know that he was stalking you."

"I don't know, but I'm going to ask him. I had told him in the past not to do anything stupid. But I doubt it. He would have told me."

"Okay! But they fucked him up."

***

Rain was home when her phone rang; it was Jordan. He wanted her to accompany him to a writing workshop at New York University. He thought she would do great. He wanted her to share her thoughts on writing and being an author. She was speechless.

"Jordan, are you serious?"

"Of course, I am. You're a very likable person. You are smart, outgoing and you know the business."

"Thanks for the kind words. I'm humbled. I don't know what to say."

"Say, yes!"

"Okay, I'll do it."

"Fantastic!"

"When is it?"

"Oh, I'm sorry. It's this coming Friday. It's from 3 to 5. Is it a problem?"

"No, it's not. I'm ecstatic."

"Good. But on another note, I heard about Melvin . . ."

"It's Matthew."

"Oh, I'm sorry. Kelly said he got beat up pretty bad and that he's in the hospital; is that right?"

"Yeah, I don't know what happened, but it was awful."

"She told me you guys visited him."

"We did."

"Did he say who did it?"

"The doctors say he has no memory of what happened that night."

There was a slight pause before he responded, "Oh, that's a shame."

"Why do you say that?"

"Because he would have been able to identify the person or persons who did it to him, but now we, I mean, no one will ever know."

"You are so right, but I hope they find out who did it."

"Good luck on . . ."

"Huh?"

"I was saying that a beautiful woman like you does not need any drama in her life. The dude is a stalker. Look how many times he's shown up. He even had the nerve to show his face when we returned from the book expo. I think he got what he deserved." Rain was silent.

"That's not a nice thing to say."

"I'm sorry. It's just that I care about you, and I hated the fact that he was doing this to you."

"Jordan, we have been through this before."

"What?"

"Where the conversation suddenly turns to me."

"My business partner is on the other line, let me call you back. If not, then Friday it is, okay; and don't forget the time. Bye."

"Okay, bye."

Rain wasn't the least comfortable with the latter part of their conversation. She wondered if he had anything to do with Matthew's hospitalization.

EPISODE

23

The assault on Matthew was deliberate and carefully planned. And, as promised, Rain wanted to know if Jerry had anything to do with it. There's a blank stare on his face as he tries to make sense of the question she asked.

"Babes, come on now. You were the one who told me what happened."

"I know, but you did mention it once, remember?"

"Sure, I did, but you convinced me not to, and so I left it alone. If you ask me, he's still a jerk."

"Jerry!"

"What? It's the truth. How did you think I felt seeing this guy, time after time, popping up?"

"I understand. But . . ."

"I'm sorry about what happened, but you can't go around stalking people. Who knows, he probably got his ass whipped from someone who he owed shit, you know what I mean?"

"I thought about that too. At least he's going to be okay."

"That's good to know; maybe he'll get it now."

"I hope so."

"So how is the writing?"

"Oh, I got an invite to speak at NYU!"

"You did?"

"Yeah, Jordan invited me."

"Oh, he did? He's another one, but I'll discuss this another time. So, what are you going to talk about?"

"You are so damn jealous, but I like that you are," she said, smiling. "Oh, I'm going to talk about self-publishing, being a writer and author; and all that I know about the business."

"That's wonderful babes; you're going to do well."

"I hope so."

"What do you mean by that?"

"I'm kind of nervous."

"Nervous? Why would you be? You talk with clients all the time. This shouldn't be any different."

"This is different; I've never spoken to a large group of people in such a setting. Jordan is expecting a large turnout. I'm worried."

"I think you will be fine. But we can do a few prep sessions if you'd like."

"That's a great idea."

***

Rain was ready as she stood in front of the sizeable crowd. Students, professors, and others from the literary world were also present. She was somewhat nervous at the outset, but with Jordan and Sandy Jenkins nodding in approval; her confidence grew; it was smooth sailing from there on in.

"Rain, you did great," Jordan said to her as the three left together.

"Guys, I have another engagement to get to," Sandy said to them. "Rain, you did wonderfully. I'll give you a call."

"Okay, Sandy, and thanks for coming."

"You're welcome. Jordan, call me later." He said he would.

"I'm starving, let's get something to eat; my treat," Jordan said.

"Sure," Rain responded.

"I know this great little place on 8th Street." While they ate, Rain had a few questions for Jordan.

"How come you never say much about yourself?"

"What do you mean?"

"You never talk about the women in your life."

Laughing, he said, "Because there's none."

"There you go with the nonsense. You know what I mean."

Getting serious, he began opening up about a past relationship that didn't turn out so well. He began by saying that she was very unassuming, beautiful, and intelligent. She had a bright future ahead of her, well-spoken and upfront. He was impressed and fell madly in love.

He had only recently embarked on his writing career. His life was in shambles as he was experiencing some hardship. She was an established executive and he felt that she would have stood by him; that was not the case. She never supported his writing career.

Hurt, he realized that he had to end the relationship. They were living together and although he did his part, most of the finances she took care of. The relationship had run its course in a short time, he went on.

"So, what did you do?" she asked him. "You moved out, or she did?"

"She did. It was good riddance as far as I was concerned."

"I know you were a happy man, weren't you?"

"You bet I was."

"So, do you see each other now?"

"No, unfortunately, she was killed."

"Oh my, I'm so sorry. How did she die? What happened?"

"She was strangled. The police said she could have been the first of the serial killer victims."

"You mean the sicko that's committing all the murders?"

"Yeah, after moving out she got an apartment on Central Park West, and you know that's where most of the women were killed."

"That's so sad. I'm sorry."

"Thanks."

"It seems you haven't gotten over it."

"Why do you say that?"

"Because of the emotion, I felt it as you spoke."

"Oh, at times I get like this. Well, enough of this. Are you ready to go?"

"Yeah, but what was her name again?"

"I never mentioned her name, but it's Jamie Rigg."

"I thought you did."

"No."

"I'm sorry. Anyways, let's go babes."

"Did you just call me, babes?"

"Yes, I did Jordan; it's a term of endearment on my part. So don't even go there," they both laughed.

***

Rain spirits were high. She never imagined things would start falling into place as quickly as they did. Jordan was steering her in the right direction, and she was more than grateful. Invited to one of his publishers' friend parties, she accepted the invite. The two were talking when a beautiful young woman approached. After introducing her to Rain, she excused herself as the two talked. It was a short conversation.

"Who is she?" Rain asked, upon returning.

"She's trying to get a book deal. She's friends with almost everyone here, but no one wants to take a chance on her, so she keeps asking me."

"So why don't you?" he stared at her as if she had lost her mind.

"What?"

"Is she a terrible writer? Not saying that she is, but why can't she get a deal?"

"I'll be honest, she cannot write."

"Wow!"

"Wow, what?"

"The way you said it that was mean."

"She can't. You want me to lie?"

"Okay, so why can't she self-published as I did?"

"She doesn't want to spend the money. She's not like me at all. Matter of fact most people aren't like me."

"What do you mean by that?"

"When opportunity knocks if I'm not there, it waits for me. That's how important I am."

He's something else, Rain thought to herself. "She needs to go the self-publish route."

"She won't and therein lies the dilemma. Not only does she want a free ride, but she wants to be a part of this group."

"So how did she get in here?"

"She knows people in the industry. See Rain, you have lots of hangers-on in this industry as well. It's very similar to the entertainment and sports industry. There are people here who are looking for more than a book deal, and some will do whatever it takes to get it. They think it's a get-rich sort of industry."

"Yeah, I've heard that."

"They believe that you write a book and that's it. No marketing. No promotion. No book signings. Nothing!"

"Are you serious?"

"Yes, I am, and she's a prime suspect."

"Wow!"

"Wow is an understatement, and when you give them the news which they dread most-which is no; they get upset and call you all sorts of names. She was trying to get in with a well-known writer friend of mine, who is also a publisher. She was trying to get her to publish her book; and when she was told that she had to come up with the finances and everything else that it entails, she made several sexual advances which were quickly rebuffed."

"Damn!"

"This is the business. But don't worry. You are in good company." She made a halfhearted attempt to smile.

EPISODE

24

It might be considered callous for everyday New Yorkers and the police to have any empathy for the Westside Serial Killer as some called him, and they had every right to feel the way they did. He had the city in a constant state of panic. No one knew when and where he would strike. It evoked an atmosphere of terror.

The police were baffled by his seemingly cold-blooded and calculated approach. Unlike mass murderers who turn themselves in, and are commonly captured or killed by law enforcement, he deliberately made special efforts to evade police officials. To him, it was a game, but to the women who lived in the neighborhood; and the police, it wasn't. They intensified their manhunt and increased their resources to the after-work locales, neighborhood bars, nightclubs, and other venues, which the mostly young and single crowd frequented.

***

They had met several months earlier on Broadway and Sixty-Seventh Street. She was using the ATM inside the Citibank on the corner. He watched her from the sidewalk. What she didn't know was how her encounter with the man watching her, would affect her life, and several of her friends.

Petite and attractive, and of Asian descent; she had a wonderful sense of warmth and innocence about her. So, when he approached her and introduced himself, she responded in kind. Telling her he was a television executive, he was quite charming and respectful, and she immediately was drawn to his personality. She ended up giving him her phone number. What she didn't know was that whenever they spoke over the phone, he was on one of his many disposable cell phones.

It wasn't long before she invited him to her apartment. On the three occasions that he visited, she had friends over as well. He would sit and chat with them. But he never stayed for an extended period. So, it wasn't strange or unusual when she saw him getting out of his car, two blocks from her apartment. They spoke for a short time before she invited him upstairs. A cool fall breeze was blowing as they walked to the building.

Once inside the apartment, she offered him a drink. He reminded her that he had to drive back home, and instead would prefer something other than alcohol.

"It's only wine. Come on, have a drink with me," she insisted.

"What the hell!" he laughed. "I guess one drink won't hurt."

He was a bit unsettled the more he drank. With his glass now empty, she offered him another. He exhibited a grandiose aura, one based on his persistent and complex narcissistic personality. His lack of empathy and compassion for someone who considers him a friend would soon play itself out.

Without warning, he began speaking incoherently. Frightened, she asked him to leave. Instead, he attacked her, snatching her by the neck. He covers her mouth and leads her into the bedroom.

"Be quiet, if you scream or try to do anything stupid, you will regret it. Do you understand me?" She nodded her head. He quickly tied her up.

"Why are you doing this to me? I thought you were my friend?"

"I am your friend, but you kept pushing me."

He was a master manipulator as he sought to keep her confused. He needed her to be unsure and doubtful.

"How so? What did I do?"

"The few times I visited, and even tonight you wanted me to drink. I didn't want to drink, but you made me."

"I'm sorry, but that wasn't my intention at all. You should have said something."

"I just did."

"I like you a lot. I only did those things because I wanted to get to know you better. I thought you were special. I was even thinking that me and you . . ."

"Stop! No! Stop saying that!"

"Saying what?"

"That I am special and that you like me. It's not true."

"But you are, and that's what attracted me to you."

"Stop! Stop saying these things." He was angry.

"What do you want me to say? You want me to lie to you?"

"No, I don't want you to lie, but . . ."

"Don't you like me?"

He avoided the question and began looking through her dresser drawers. Taking a pair of her panties and a scarf, he approached her. She began sobbing.

"Please don't do this to me," she cried, uncontrollably.

It was then that it dawned on her that he was the Westside Killer. She was about to scream when he lunged at her, his huge hands covering her mouth. Stuffing the panty in her mouth, he calmly put the scarf around her neck and strangled her.

"I never wanted you," he muttered.

He was deliberate as he removed her clothes and left her lifeless body in the room.

Hours later

He sat transfixed in front of the mirror as if waiting for a response of satisfaction or to be scolded. He didn't display any emotion.

'I did it. Are you satisfied?' he said, with an odd look on his face. *'I did as you said, but I want you to know that I had a difficult time doing it.'*

'How so?'

'She said she liked me.'

'And you believed her? How stupid are you?'

'I am not stupid. You need to stop saying that. And why are you laughing?'

'Because she didn't; it was nothing but a ploy.'

'No, it wasn't. She cared about me. You do this to me all the time.'

'You need to stop being so naive.'

'Can't I love somebody?'

'Love? She wasn't any different.'

'*You are wrong. She wasn't a bad girl. She wasn't like the others. I felt something for her. Yes, I did. Stop laughing at me. Will you stop fucking laughing at me?*'

'*You are pathetic. You are nothing. You can't even think for yourself.*'

'*Yes, I can. Okay, I'm sorry. I know you are my best friend and the only one who cares about me.*'

'*It would be best to keep that in mind.*'

'*I will. I'm going now. No, you haven't been wrong, and you haven't let me down. I'm going in the shower now.*' He had an amused look on his face as he got up off the floor.

EPISODE

25

Released from the hospital after several months, and resting at home, a fearful Matthew had no recollection of his assailants, and this troubled him. Several of his co-workers visited, including Kelly. It worried him that Rain hadn't shown up, but he was optimistic that she would. When she finally did, he was thrilled. They discussed a few things. She asked if he knew who his attackers were, and like he told the others, the answer was no.

"For most of my life, I have been a given person. I have given my time, my patience; and my know-how to all who needed it. I have no enemies. Why they did this to me is beyond me. It pains me deeply."

"I'm so sorry that this happened to you. I know you're a great guy, Matt."

"Thanks, babes. Maybe I need to be in this situation more often, it seems it's the only way I'll hear any kind words from you," he said, laughing.

She couldn't help but laugh, "You shouldn't say that. That's not cool at all."

"I know, that's why I said it. How are things at work?"

"Well, other than everybody waiting for your crazy ass to return, it's the same shit. Why you expect a miracle to take place?"

"That will be the day, but on another note, Kelly said there's a new guy on the job. Is it true?"

"Yeah, his cubicle is next to hers. They are cool."

"What do you mean by cool?"

"They like each other."

"Oh, she didn't say shit about that."

"He's a pretty cool guy. His name is Blair Stratton."

"You mean Blair as in Blair Underwood?"

"Yeah," she said, laughing.

"I don't know too many brothers with that name."

"Me neither. But they seem to be an item."

"I see. Is he checking you out?"

"I don't know, but if he is, that's his problem."

Laughing, he said, "Cos you've still got me to deal with. I'm the only man for you and you know it.

"I don't know about all that. What I do know is that you're a pain in the ass."

"You got me this way, but on another note, I'm glad that you came."

"Regardless of what we went through in our relationship, I still care about you. I didn't like what happened and if you must know, I still care about you, despite all the shit you put me through."

"Thanks, Rain, and I feel the same, but what do you mean by all the shit?" They both laughed.

"Don't worry about it, it's nothing. But there's something I need to tell you."

"What is it?"

"It's Linda."

"What about her?"

"She's dead. The police think it's the Westside Killer."

"Damn, that's fucked up. I spoke to her a while back and she said she was doing great."

"She told me and Kelly the same thing. She had met some guy, but she said she was taking it slowly, and now this."

"That's some bullshit. Linda was a nice person."

"I know. I'm gonna miss her."

"It seems all my fucking friends are dying. What the fuck is going on? They need to catch that mutha-fucka. He's wreaking havoc."

"I know. Maybe I shouldn't have said anything about it to you."

"What are you talking about? It's cool. I'll be alright."

"I know you guys were great friends . . ."

"Say no more, it's cool. I'll be alright."

"Well okay, but I gotta go, but I'll be in touch."

"Cool. I appreciate you coming," he said. They hugged.

***

Blair Stratton began working at Le Chic soon after Matthew's hospitalization. Thirty-two years old and single, he was bright and ambitious; not to mention his boyish good looks. Charmed by his good looks, he and Kelly quickly hit it off. It wasn't long before they were an item. Although they had only been seeing each other for a short time, it seemed like forever. As for Rain, she was under the impression that Kelly and Tatyana were still an item. She didn't say much about it.

Sometime thereafter, Kelly began inviting him to several of Rain's book signings. She eventually introduced him to Jordan and Jerry. It was at one of Jordan's parties that Blair was approached by a young man who thought he looked familiar.

"I think you have the wrong person," he said to the young man.

"I guess you must have a twin."

"Maybe, my dad was a rolling stone, so it's possible." The men burst out in laughter and dap each other before going their separate ways.

"That guy you saw me talking to, he's a real character," Blair said to Kelly.

"What do you mean?"

"He's telling me he knows me from somewhere. I told him you have the wrong guy. This mutha-fucka said I have a twin. I told him my dad was a rolling stone, so it was possible. That shit had him cracking up."

"You're crazy," she said laughing.

"Í know. That I am," he smiled, nodding his head, as they walked over to where Rain and Jordan were sitting.

***

"Mother, what is it now?"

"Is that how you greet your mother? Darling, I haven't heard from you in two weeks."

"Mother, we spoke a few nights ago."

"We did? Oh, yes, that's right. How can I forget? I have been so into Fifi at times I forget simple things."

"Still haven't cleared the air with grandma?"

"Darling, she does have a mouth you know."

"Mother, stop it!"

"Are you going to keep asking me this question . . .?"

"Yes, when you clear the air with her, then I will stop. You'll apologize to Fifi before apologizing to your mother, is that it?"

"Not at all, but I promise I will."

"You say that all the time."

"I will. By the way, how are things between you and that rich boyfriend of yours? Oh, and he's very handsome." She giggled.

Rain could only smile. "Everything is fine!"

"Wonderful! I know he's not like that worthless ex-husband of yours."

"No mother, the divorce hasn't been finalized as yet. I know that's why you called."

"But darling, what's a mother to do? You are my child and I want the best for you."

"I know that mom, but . . ."

"But what?"

"I know you want what's best for me, but at times you go above and beyond."

"I do?"

"Yes, you do."

"Well, I apologize. I'm sorry."

"It's okay." The two spoke at length about family and friends, and as they ended their conversation, her mother said Jerry was a great catch, to which Rain responded, "I know, that's why I'm holding on to him." The two laughed.

"Talk to you later, sweetheart," her mother said, hanging up.

***

Jerry met Rain at her apartment as she asked him. He was in a wonderful mood as he playfully slapped her on the butt. She returned the favor and soon they were in bed making passionate love. After their sexual romp, Jerry sat her down. He had a few things he wanted to discuss.

"Remember the night at my place?" he asked, sitting up in the bed.

"Which night?" she asked with a smile.

"The night we played ball."

"Yeah, what about it?"

"You told me you were married, right?"

"Yeah."

"So, what's the situation . . . you know, like what's going on?"

"I'm waiting for him to do the right thing."

"Which is?"

"Getting the paperwork done."

"Okay, but what I'm about to tell you, is something you need to hear and know."

"Whatever it is, why didn't you tell me this earlier?" Rain couldn't help but think of her situation, but she wanted to hear the rest of what he had to say.

"I didn't think the timing was right."

"So, what makes it right now?"

"Because you are waiting for your divorce to be finalized and I just believe that now is the right time."

Smiling, she said, "Fair enough."

"It's about my ex-wife."

"Your ex-wife? You were married?" the look on her face could have stopped Jason Voorhees from the Friday The 13th movie series in his tracks.

Not paying much attention to her reaction, Jerry continued, "Yeah. It was problematic."

"Go on," Rain said, interestingly.

We were in love at least I was. She was quite the lady, smart, beautiful, and educated. She had her own catering business, which was doing great. She had quite an upscale clientele. She was full of promises. Upon meeting her, I was smitten. I was more than impressed with her overall career choices. But the thing that impressed me the most and had a lasting impression on me, was her astute good-heartedness for others."

"What do you mean? What did she do?"

"She was involved with some charities."

"That was nice of her. But go on."

"We fell madly in love with each other. Perhaps it was too fast, but we didn't care. There was a seven-year difference between us." Rain had a half-hearted smile on her face. "It wasn't long before we were engaged and then married."

"How long were you married?"

"Three years. Things got worse when we got married. It was a living hell, to say the least."

"What did she do that was so bad?"

"She stole thousands of dollars from my family business."

"Are you serious?"

"Yes, I am. She manipulated the paperwork, and I never suspected a thing."

"Who did?"

"My dad began noticing certain discrepancies and began monitoring them. It wasn't long before his investigation led to her, and when confronted she denied everything."

"So, what happened? You divorced her and moved on?"

"Hell no, we did get divorced but only after her ass was arrested."

"She was arrested?"

"Oh yeah, she's still in jail. She was sentenced to 15 years."

"Oh shit, are you serious?"

"Yes, I am. I'm not lying. She was held accountable and had to pay the penalty for what she did."

"Okay! I understand."

"See, this is what happens when you rush into things, and this is what happened with me and her. The thing is, I thought we could accomplish some things together. But she had an agenda, and it didn't include me."

"You can say that again. But that's crazy; I have never heard anything like that in my life. I'm guessing it was on the news given it happened to your father?"

"Yes, it was. It was all over the place."

"I can imagine."

"This is why I took so long to share this with you."

"I get it. You wanted to be sure about me, right?"

"Sure, I did. I have to be honest with you. But what I noticed immediately was that you weren't wide-eyed or consumed with the fact that my father was wealthy. I admire you for that. You didn't even know who my father was." He laughed.

"Yup, I sure didn't. I was from another world."

He stared at her. She blushed. A chill came over her. He held her hands and said, "I want to marry you as soon as your divorce is finalized. You can take some time to think it over, but I'm sure that you are the one. It wasn't by happenstance that we met. It was destiny."

"Don't say that!" she said, tearing up.

"And why not?"

"Because."

"I don't get it."

"It isn't anything bad. It's just that my life isn't where I want it to be at this point."

"Guess what? You and I can get it to the point where you'd like it to be. How about that?"

She bit her bottom lip and looked into his eyes. He did the same. It seemed like forever as she slowly and deliberately uttered the words. "I love you, Jerry. But can I take some time and think about it?"

"Of course, you can. We're not going to rush into this without thinking it through."

"Okay, babes, I will let you know. Oh, did I mention the young Asian girl?"

"The one who recently died?"

"Yes, her."

"What about her?"

"I want you to look into something for me."

"What do you mean? I'm not a cop."

"I know that, but I want you to see if you can get any information about her death. The police haven't been saying anything of late and she was a friend."

"I'll see what I can do, but I can't promise you anything."

"I understand, but try, please."

"For you, okay." He smiled.

EPISODE

26

Growing up in Nanuet, New York, he was like most youngsters. He played sports and chased girls. He was an exceptional student and graduated second in his high school class. He attended college but dropped out in his sophomore year. He had a few friends. Friendly to some extent, he was viewed by some of his classmates as strange. Yet, there weren't any reasons to raise an alarm. Years later, his parents would find a troubling letter that he wrote to an anonymous friend.

The letter read:

You thought I was nothing more than a pawn in your grand scheme of things. I didn't know where to turn when you walked out on me. Yet I knew our many conversations wouldn't let you just walk away and forget about me.

We have been friends as far back as I can recall, kids; that's what we were. I knew you were prepared to take flight, but where and how you would get there troubled me deeply. Yet I never doubt that I will see you again. My nights were sleepless. I was restless. I know you are probably wondering why I took the time to write this letter after all that you have done for me. You took me for granted? Yes, you did. The truth is, I allowed it to happen. I never tried to stop you, or did I? I can't recall. Maybe once or twice, that's it. You never thought I was crazy, but I thought you were. Whenever they made fun of me, they made fun of you as well. Remember the day you and I were by the lake when Allison Macintosh passed us on her way to go to the summer fair? I know you remember because it was our first time kissing a girl and seeing it. Your eyes lit up when you saw it. I did too. It was our first experience together.

It was soon after our encounter with Allison that we made a pact. We never lied to her and neither did she. She wanted it, and we gave it to her. She never complained and she never told on us. You know the others thought we were weird, didn't you? They would mock us, but we never revealed how we felt about them and the worthless, infantile, egotistical, stupid, and unwarranted friendship they offered. They were nothing more than attention seekers. They desired the spotlight and craved it and we gave it to them, didn't we? Yes, sir, we did. It was great hearing from you, and I promise I will stay in contact. Until we meet again . . . I shouldn't say that, ignore it. What I should say is that I cannot wait until we are in each other's presence.

Love, Me

It never crossed his parent's minds to look deeper into what he wrote and why, and to who he wrote it. Instead, they summed it up as innocent adolescent shenanigans. Years later, the letter was lost in a fire when his parents died. The letter was very important because it detailed his encounter with Allison Macintosh, his first victim.

***

Matthew has been feeling much better since his release from the hospital. He was homesick and wanted to get back to work. He tried to convince his supervisors he was well, but they would have none of it. His health was more important, and they reminded him of it. Nonetheless, the days leading up to his return to work, saw him visiting more often. His co-workers were happy to see him and welcomed him with open arms.

"Is this the new guy?" he asked Rain, pointing at Blair.

"Yes, that's him. Come, let me introduce you." She did.

"He seems like a cool cat."

"He is. I guess you won't be pushing up on Kelly anymore." She laughed.

"Come on Rain, don't do me like that."

"Matt, you will fuck anything in a skirt and that includes me and Kelly and all the women that are in this office."

"See, you fucked up."

"What do you mean?"

"It's all the women in the building."

"You are so damn nasty." They both laughed.

"I can't wait to get back to work. Where's Kelly?"

"She left early. She wasn't feeling well."

"Oh, okay, I'm gonna give her a call and stop by."

"Okay! You take care and get well." She hugged him.

"I will."

***

"How could you mislead me and do such a horrible thing?" a pissed Rain angrily shouted, storming into Jerry's Manhattan office.

"What are you talking about?"

"I can't believe you would stoop to such levels . . ."

"What are you talking about?" he repeated.

"Matt. Why did you send those guys to beat him up? I told you not to get involved. We spoke about it a number of times and you said that you wouldn't. So why did you do it?"

"Who told you that I had something to do with it? Where did you get that from?"

"Baby, stop! I know you had it done."

"Look, he had it coming to him. He was a pain in the ass. Everywhere we went he showed up. What man is going to tolerate shit like that? He was a damn nuisance."

"We spoke about it, and I begged you not to hurt him. They could have killed him, and they almost did."

He didn't know what to say as she became teary-eyed. "I'm sorry. You are right. I get it. I shouldn't have done it."

"He's my friend, Jerry. What we had is in the past, but he's a nice person. They shouldn't have done that to him. It pained me to see him like that, and now, knowing that you were involved hurts even more."

"I was only trying to get him off our backs. It shouldn't have turned out as it did. They were only supposed to rough him up. I apologize. Can you forgive me? You don't have to answer me now." The look on her face said she would. She was heading for the door when he called her.

"What now, Jerry?"

"How did you know it was me?"

"I overheard you on the phone talking with one of your buddies and you looked at me twice as I slept before talking in a hush, and it was the same night that I brought him up. I wasn't sleeping. But I wasn't sure if it was you until I asked the person you were on the phone with."

"You did? You asked Jack and he told you this?"

"Yes, he did."

He clasped his hands and apologized once again. She didn't know what to make of it. "Oh!"

"What is it, Jerry?"

"It's about your friend. My sources said she was dating several guys. The police questioned them, but they were later released, which means they weren't the killers. So, if I was a betting man, I would say the killer is still out there."

"I appreciate you looking into it for me. It's so sad. I miss her. But there was a guy she was seeing, I can't remember his name, but she spoke about him a lot. I don't know if he's one of the guys that the cops had in their custody and let go, but you never know."

"I can tell that her death has affected you. Whoever this guy is if he's still around, he should speak to the authorities, you know what I mean?"

"Yeah. It makes a lot of sense."

"Maybe he's one of the guys they let go. You never know."

Sighing, she hoped for the best. "I'm sorry for speaking to you as I did."

"It's okay. I was wrong. Let's put it behind us, deal?"

"Deal."

With the unsolved death of her friend on her mind, she remained confident that the police would arrest the killer sooner rather than later. Although no one talks about her death at work, it doesn't ease their pain seeing someone else in her cubicle. At the same time, the thought of telling Matthew who was behind his attack never crossed her mind. She knew it would be a mistake. As for Kelly, she was stunned when told.

EPISODE
27

She recently arrived in New York City and reached out to Rain through a mutual friend. New to the city, she thought it was best to stay with friends rather than at a hotel. Financially, she was okay, but with the stories she heard about the city, some good, some not so good — she thought it was in her best interest to contact Rain. Several mishaps led to her losing contact with her, so she was more than relieved when the mutual friend they shared, reached out to her.

A beautiful blonde, Ashley Simmons needed a career change and she felt New York was the ideal place. A year younger than Rain, she's hoping for a new start, and the bond the two share is something she's looking forward to. So, when she contacted her, she was more than willing to give her a helping hand. The two women had been friends since they were introduced by Jonathan soon after their marriage. She soon realized that Jonathan basically controlled her every move and that she was constantly in fear for her life. Following a heated argument one night, Rain fled their home and spent the night at Ashley's place. Whenever she and Jonathan argued that's where she would go.

"I'm so happy to see you."

"Me too," Rain replied.

"You look great."

"Thanks, and you don't look so bad yourself."

"Girl, I have been taking care of myself. I can't afford to let myself go like some of these women."

"I know that's right, girl."

"What's been going on in Michigan since I left?"

"Not much, it's the same old thing. But Jonathan has himself a new girlfriend."

"He does, huh?"

"Yes, he does."

"Hmm, I see."

"Girl, she has nothing on you."

"I know that." Rain smiled.

"I saw him at a function a few months ago and he was rather rude."

"What do you mean?"

"He was saying some harsh things about you; and that he'll do the paperwork when he's good and ready."

"Was he speaking to only you?"

"No, we were in a small group of at least eight people."

"I defended you and he got really angry at me. You know how he can get."

"I know exactly what you mean."

The women spoke at length and Rain filled her in on the events that have taken place in her life. Ashley was more than happy to hear the good news.

***

Ashley was from a well-to-do neighborhood in Michigan. She was born with a silver spoon in her mouth, so to speak. Her friends thought she was a snob, but they were moochers, and they loved the attention. She was popular in high school and was captain of the cheerleading team. Parties, boys, fast cars, and getting high were what mattered to her. She was a rebel or so she thought. Her small but loyal tight-knit group of friends jumped at her every whim. It continued right up until she entered college, where she was admitted into the bachelor's and master's programs. There a sudden transformation took place. Those who knew her from her high school days were surprised at the sudden change.

Her parents were elated. She had grown up. They thought she was on the right path, especially her father who loved her dearly. After graduation, and armed with a degree in forensic psychology, she moved to California, where she was hired by the City's Forensic Department. Well-respected by her peers, a team player, and a hard worker, she loved her job.

She soon fell in love with a much older married man. Their relationship was an abusive one. Warned by friends to get out of the situation after being rushed to the hospital with a mild concussion and several cracked ribs; she finally broke off the relationship. Although she remained in California after being released from the hospital, she was very depressed. After several relationships, none of which went well, she decided to return home. She moved in with her parents who welcomed her with open arms. Soon thereafter, her mother took control of her life as she fought depression. Her mother had a huge influence on her life. It certainly wasn't an amicable relationship.

Her father's empathy was well received because it meant everything to her. With her depression getting worse, he sought help for her. She soon began seeing a doctor twice a month and began making some progress, but for whatever reason, her mother wasn't a willing supporter. She always felt that her husband paid her a lot more attention than he did her. She became a thorn in her life. Ashley recovered enough to eventually move out. Her mother was against it, but her father thought she was ready, and he was right.

It was after moving out that she ran into Jonathan, a longtime acquaintance. After meeting Rain, the two women became fast friends and began working out at the local gym — one of the few places Jonathan allowed her. Ashley was one of the few friends that were allowed into their home. The women had more in common than they would ever realize.

She witnessed the abuse first-hand, and after telling Rain what she had gone through; she was constantly in her ear. Rain was horrified at the things she shared, and after some time she built up the nerves to walk away.

***

Matthew was glad to be back at work. His co-workers were happy to see him. Blair had a reserved look on his face as he observed them. But a change was coming, that would surprise the office, but especially Rain and Kelly. As the weeks passed, the once standoffish behavior between the two was a thing of the past. They had become friends, more like old friends.

"How are things with you and Blair?" Rain asked Matthew one afternoon at work.

"What do you mean? We're cool. He seems like a cool dude."

"I told you. I knew you two would get along."

"What's this some kind of 'I want you and Blair to get along' type of shit?"

Laughing, she said, "No not at all, it's just that the brother is cool, and you are too, and it will keep you from bothering and getting on me and Kelly's nerves."

"Damn, that's how you see me? That's fucked up. I can't believe my ex is trying to get rid of me."

"No, I'm not. I'm just saying though."

"What are you saying?" he said, as Kelly approached.

"Who is saying what?" Kelly butts in.

"Rain just told me that you guys were hoping that me and Blair would hit it off, so I would leave y'all alone. Am I that much of a pain in the ass?"

"Oh, she did?" she asked, laughing. "You do be getting on our last nerves at times, but we love you though. But it's good that you and Blair are cool."

"That's exactly what I said to him," Rain smiled.

"Man, I gotta get away from you two." The three laughed before getting back to work.

"Oh, I almost forgot, Jerry is having a get-together next weekend and I want you guys there." Turning to Blair she said, "Can I have a word with you?" she asked him, as he approached.

"Hey, y'all, what is it, Rain?"

"My boyfriend and I are having a get-together and I wanna know if you would like to . . .?"

"Of course, he's coming," Kelly said, cutting her off.

Rain smiled as Matthew and Blair chuckled.

Things didn't go so well with Jordan who refused initially. It was only at Rain and Kelly's urging that he agreed. As for Blair, it was a go, because of Kelly. However, Rain had to get the go-ahead from Jerry.

***

The following week couldn't come any sooner as Kelly, Matthew, Blair, and Jordan showed up for the party. Jerry had a shocked look on his face when he saw Matthew. His mind was racing. He wondered if he knew he was responsible for what happened to him. Besides, he wasn't sure if Rain discussed it with him. She did promise she wouldn't say a word about it. Yet he was a bit uneasy. Rain quickly picked up on it and assured him she hadn't said a word. He pulled her aside.

"Why didn't you tell me that you invited him? You never mentioned him. You told me about Jordan and Boo, Blair, whatever the fuck his name is, but not him."

"I felt it would be better this way. He doesn't know. I'm at fault. I am. I kept it from you. I shouldn't have. As for him knowing, no, we discussed the matter a few days ago and I made it clear to you, that I never mentioned or discussed anything about it with him." Despite Rain's reassurance about Matthew, Jerry was worried he could face an assault charge if he found out he was responsible. The threat of jail loomed over his head, and it was something he was uncomfortable with.

"Fair enough, but you discussed it with Kelly? I know you," he stated.

"Yeah, she's the only one."

"But what if she said something?"

"No, she didn't. I'm sure."

"Okay, I'm gonna take your word for it."

"Yes, do that, because you have no other choice," she teased. "But you know you're terrible?"

"How so?"

"You said Boo, Blair, whatever the fuck his name is, that shit was funny." They were laughing when Blair, Jordan, and Matthew walked over.

"This is a great place you have here," Blair said to Jerry.

"Thanks, brother, and feel free to partake of whatever you like."

"Thanks, I appreciate it."

"No problem. Hey, Matt, how are you doing?"

"I'm doing great. I'm feeling much better."

"That's wonderful."

"It's great seeing you."

"Likewise," Jerry replied. He had some remorse as they talked. "Enjoy yourself and have fun."

"I sure will."

"Hey, Jerry, how are things with you?" Kelly asked.

Smiling, he said, "I'm doing great, and you?"

"The same as you." She returned his smile.

Jordan wasn't saying much. Other than a hello, he brushed Jerry off. His attention was on Rain, Kelly, and the other stylishly dressed women.

EPISODE

28

Blair was glad he accepted the invite. It was unlike anything he had ever been around. There were several influential people whom he came in contact with. He and Jordan were making the rounds when Matthew approached them. He didn't say much to Jordan as he and Blair spoke. Their conversation was short, and the two men continued.

"Isn't she lovely?" Jordan said to Blair, pointing to a beautiful young woman. She was having a conversation with an older woman.

"No doubt about it. You better introduce yourself or I will," he playfully said.

"But aren't you dating, Kelly?"

"Yeah. But shit like that you can't let pass you by. You know what I mean?"

"Damn bro, you sound just like me. I'm not mad at you at all."

"I hear you. But like I said, you better introduce yourself."

"I'll be right back." He walked towards the two women. "Excuse me, but can I offer you a drink?" he said, eyeballing both women.

"I believe I am much too old for you, young man," the older of the two women responded.

Bemused, his sense of humor quickly surfaced. "Surely, you are not. You look rather young," he said, getting the attention of a young woman serving the guests. He handed both women a drink.

Smiling, the younger woman thanked him. "And what is your name young man?" the older woman asked.

"Jordan."

"Jordan? Is that it? You don't have a surname?"

The smile on his face quickly disappeared. "I'm sorry, it's Jordan Jagger."

"My, what a wonderful name. I'm Ruth Benjamin and this is my niece, Janet Dawson."

Jordan was speechless. "You're Jerry's, mother?"

"Well, I gave birth to him not unless you know something that I don't," she said, laughing.

"I'm so sorry."

"Sorry for what?"

"I didn't know . . ."

"Hush . . . it's fine," she said, cutting him off. "Young man, what kind of work do you do, if you don't mind me asking?"

"I'm a writer and author."

"Oh, how wonderful, and what kind of books do you write? Any scholarly works?"

"No ma'am, not at all. I write fiction."

"There's no need to refer to me as ma'am. I can see that you are quite a respectable young man, and it makes me sound way much older than I am." She let out a hearty laugh. "So, what kind of fiction is it?"

"Suspense, crime, and romance."

"That is wonderful. Perhaps I'll be fortunate enough to read one of your books. Matter of fact, I think I will. What are the titles . . . better yet, give them to my niece? I'll leave you two alone, but I'll be keeping an eye on you, Mr. Jordan." She took a sip from her glass and left them alone.

Blair, from where he stood, watched the whole thing unfold. It was only when Ruth left the two alone, did he focused his attention elsewhere.

***

"Hey, isn't that Jordan with your cousin?" Rain whispered to Jerry.

"Oh?"

"Yes, take a look."

"Okay, it's him and?"

"Aren't you gonna say something to him?"

"For what?"

"Because you know how he is, and it's your cousin."

"She's grown and just so you know, she's not that naïve. I'll talk to her later. There's no harm being done right now; they are just talking."

"Wow! But we are talking about Jordan, the man who has never seen a skirt that he doesn't like."

"No shit, I'm joking, babes. But I'll take care of it — if it will make you feel better."

"Thank you, and yes, it will make me feel much better."

Minutes later, Blair was talking with Kelly when Jordan approached. He was having fun and it showed.

"Can I hang with you guys for a second?"

"Sure," Blair said.

"I was just leaving," Kelly added, walking away.

"Did you know the older lady that I was talking to was Jerry's, mother and the shapely girl is his cousin?"

"Oh really, I kind of sense something was wrong. I thought you were trying to get his mother's number." Both men laughed.

"She's a very nice lady though."

"I see, but how did it go with the cousin?"

"She took my number. I hope Jerry doesn't have a problem with it. You know how those rich guys get at times."

"I hear you. But you believe he would say something?"

"I don't know. But when I first met Rain, I tried to get with her. He quickly made it known that she was off-limits."

"Dude, that's his woman. You ought to expect that. But this is his cousin that's different."

"You're right. We'll see though."

"The most she can do is not call, right?"

"Yeah, that's a valid point. You're right."

"Hey, what's up with you and Matt? I noticed you guys don't talk much."

"I don't fuck with him. He's got that stalker shit about him."

"What do you mean?"

"He used to date Rain and she dumped him. This was a few years ago but they remained friends. Seems he hasn't gotten over her. He showed up unannounced while she was with Jerry. He showed up at several of my book signings."

"Hmm, was she with you at the signings?"

"Indeed. I wanted to kick his ass, but Rain told me not to go there."

Laughing, he said, "Are you sure you weren't the one who sent him to the hospital?" Blair laughed.

"Nope, but I wasn't upset."

"So, he's on Rain shit like that?"

"Absolutely. It's only recently that he's toned it down. Oh, see that blonde standing next to Rain and Kelly?"

"Yeah, what about her?"

"That's Rain's girlfriend. Her name is Ashley Simmons. She recently relocated from Michigan and from what I've heard she's been dating him."

"That's cool, maybe now he'll leave Rain alone."

"Let's hope so. So how are things going with you and that fine woman, Kelly?"

He never saw the glare that Blair gave him, before responding, "We've got a good thing going. Yes, we do."

"That's cool. You know I've known her for the longest?"

"Really?"

"Yeah, I had a crush on her back in the day, but she turned me down. You're a lucky man."

Blair smiled, "I guess I am. I showed up at the right time, huh?"

"I guess you did, but enough about this. Let's see what the women are up to."

"Kelly and Rain are right there with a group of women."

"Brother, I'm not talking about them. I'm talking about the group of women standing over there."

"Oh, I didn't see them, but you go ahead. I'll catch up with you."

"You sure you don't want me to wait for you?"

"It's cool; go ahead, I'll be with you in a few."

"Okay, brother!"

Blair never met up with him as he promised. He spends the rest of the night with Kelly, Rain, and Ashley. Jordan thought nothing of it. They all had a wonderful time. Jerry did talk to his niece and politely told her to keep their relationship on a friendship basis. He advised her to not make it so obvious.

It wasn't long before Jordan got the message, and he didn't take it kindly. He saw himself as every woman's dream and Janet's ill-treatment of him shattered his ego. Moreover, he feared a confrontation with Jerry would be inevitable if he continued to pursue her, and that was something he didn't want.

EPISODE

29

Kelly and Blair's relationship had blossomed in the short time they had been seeing each other. She wanted more than just a typical boyfriend-girlfriend relationship, so she asked him to move in with her. It was a bold move on her part, but it was something she was ready for and wanted.

"I'm not saying that I don't want to, but I don't think it's a good idea at the moment," Blair said to her. They were at his apartment.

"So, I'll move in with you then." He didn't respond. "Not even that?" she asked with an uneasy look on her face.

"It's just that . . ."

"What?"

"Remember the conversation you and I had a while back about the girl I dated a few years ago, the one who lived out of state?"

"Okay, what about her?"

"She put me through some shit. The shit was unfathomable."

"What happened?"

"You're not going to believe this."

"Why wouldn't I? Try me."

"She asked me if I would relocate, and I said sure. She said she loved me, and I believed her."

"Did you love her?"

"I did. Anyways, I agreed to relocate and joined her in Miami."

"What kind of job did she have?"

"She was into real estate."

"Hmm!"

"For almost two months she and I were living it up. She had a nice house with all the amenities given her occupation. One night, we were in the tv room watching a movie, I can't recall what it was; when I heard the keys and the alarm went off. I thought someone was breaking in, so I jumped up and ran to the kitchen and grabbed a knife, hoping that the police would show up. But guess what?

An elderly woman walked in, said hi to us, and turned to my girlfriend and said, 'I took care of the alarm already.' I was dumbfounded. 'Who the fuck was that?' I asked her after the lady left."

"Don't tell me it's what I'm thinking?"

"You got that right; it was her mother. I said you live with your mother, and you didn't tell me . . .?"

"Wow!"

"Wait, it gets better. She was about to respond when the lady called her. I overheard the lady telling her that it was her house that she pays the mortgage and that she didn't want any stranger in her house. I was stunned."

"Damn, are you fucking serious?"

"Yeah, she was pleading her case though."

"What did she say?"

"She was telling her mother that the upstairs penthouse was hers, that she also contributed to the mortgage, and that she was a grown woman. Her mother shot back, 'Well since you're a grown woman then you and your friend, I'm assuming he's your boyfriend, get the fuck out of my house.' Speechless wasn't the word, I was fucked. Here I was thinking that she and I were about to start and build a life together. I relocated because I trusted her. She said she loved me. This was supposed to be a good thing for both of us. She convinced me that the house belonged to her. I never questioned it."

"Wow!"

"There's more!"

"Hmm!"

"I would later find out that she hadn't worked in the past year and a half. She was laid off. So, she was living off her savings. She had some money saved. It's not like she was broke, she was far from it . . ."

"What did she say to you?"

"She kept crying and telling me how sorry she was and asked for my forgiveness. I forgave her, but I was angry, angry that she lied. She could have and should have told me the truth. But she chose to fabricate shit to get me to Florida. It's not like I wouldn't have visited, I just wouldn't have relocated at the time that I did. I would have waited, but she kept pushing the issue, and ever since that happened, I promised myself that I wouldn't let that happen to me ever again."

"That was fucked up. She's a fucked-up person. Seemed she was a good girl, but she lied."

"She was a nice girl, but lying, that's the thing that will change my outlook pretty quick in a relationship."

"Yeah, it will."

"So, I hope you understand. I'm not saying that you are gonna lie."

"I know what you mean. I understand."

"I'm glad you do. I love you Kelly and I know the feelings are mutual, but we'll know when to move in together. Is that cool with you?"

"It's cool."

Days later

"Hey, Tatyana, how are you and how is the weather treating you?"

"I'm fine and fuck the weather!" She was pissed.

"What's wrong?"

"You know what's wrong."

"No, I don't."

"So, when were you going to tell me about that wanna-be broke-ass, Blair Underwood?"

"I was, and I'm sorry I didn't mention it to you earlier."

"That's fucked up. I thought we had something?"

"We did."

"Could have fooled me!"

"But you're there and I'm here, and I would get bored at times."

"How did you think I felt?"

"Okay, but I didn't see you breaking your neck to get down here."

"And neither did you."

"Whatever. Was it your sister who told you about him?"

"No, I have other sources."

"So, tell me."

"Don't worry about who the person is. You should have told me what was going on?"

"You know what?"

"What?"

"I'm gonna be upfront and honest with you."

"Okay, go ahead."

"Our relationship was not working, and you know that."

"I did, huh?"

"Yes, and I felt it was time to move on."

"If you felt this way, why didn't you just tell me?"

"You're right, I should have."

"I didn't think you would treat me this way."

"I'm truly sorry."

"I don't know what you were thinking."

"Okay, here's the deal. Yes, I'm seeing Blair and we are in love. We plan on moving in together."

"Wow! You guys are serious, huh?"

"Yeah, I love him."

"I didn't know you guys were that far ahead of the eight ball."

"I guess we are."

"I see."

"But you are still my best friend."

"Hmm."

"I don't like the sound of that."

"Why? You want me to jump for joy?"

"No, but I want you to be happy for me."

"Who says I'm not?"

"It doesn't sound like it."

"Well, I am. I'm happy for you, but . . ."

"But what?"

"The way how you went about it."

"I said I was sorry, and I apologize."

"Are you aware that I'm in town?"

"You are?"

"Yes, I am."

"Rain knows that you're here?"

"Not yet, but she will soon."

"So where are you?"

"I'm at Ashley's apartment."

"Her new place? I didn't know you guys were friends."

"Yup. We are."

"So, was it her who told you?"

"Told me what?"

"Blair!"

"If you must know it was her."

"I see."

"Please don't start anything with her."

"I won't."

"She doesn't know about us."

"She doesn't?"

"No! We were just talking, and he came up."

"Okay, cool. So, are you coming to see me?"

"Why?"

"Will you stop it? I want to see you."

"Okay, remember that spot we used to hang out at?"

"Yes, I remember."

"Let's meet there in an hour."

"See you then."

The two met as planned and chatted for a short time. After a few drinks, they ended up in Kelly's apartment. Knowing Blair would call, Kelly called him instead. Convinced she was working on a project for work, he said he understood. Tatyana looked on with a sheepish smile. There wasn't much talking between them after the call ended. Tatyana pulled Kelly close. They kissed. Their roaming tongues dug deep into each other throats.

Within minutes they were naked. Their swollen nipples rubbed against each other, driving them wild. Their arousing breaths sent shivers down their necks. Their hands caressed their asses before finding their honey spot. They shrieked in ecstasy as their fingers now soaked from their juice slid in and out of their secret garden. They moaned as they straddled each other. They needed some tongue action, and they proceeded — satisfying each other. Their moans were subtle and sensual as they raced in a slow-motion bliss, squeezing and biting, as their tongues drove them to a blistering climax. After showering and getting dressed, their mood was nothing like their earlier conversation. They were laughing and making jokes. Not once was Blair's name mentioned. The two left the apartment together. Kelly went to meet Blair, and Tatyana headed to Ashley's place.

EPISODE

30

Rain was at work when her lawyer called and told her to stop by his office. She had a lot on her mind as she left work. She knew it had to do with her divorce. Taking a seat, she was thrilled upon hearing that Jonathan had signed the divorce papers. It wasn't too long ago that she sent the divorce papers via first-class mail, along with a form of acknowledgment for him to sign; despite telling everyone she had done so a while back. All the same, it took Jonathan sometime before he cooperated. The authorities had to get involved and he was ordered in front of a judge. It was only then that he signed the papers.

A settlement was agreed upon relating to the assets and maintenance of their time together as a married couple. Surprisingly enough, Rain was given the condo in downtown Detroit, and two luxury cars, one of which was a Lexus coupe. She was also given a hefty sum and a percentage of his stocks and bonds. Jonathan was livid. It was only at the urging of his lawyer that he came to his senses. He was reminded that the judge wouldn't have let her walk away empty-handed.

She was ecstatic upon hearing the news. She called her mother and told her. She was elated.

"I'm glad it's over with. He treated you terribly and you deserved every damn penny. I only wanted what was best for you and nothing more."

"I know mother."

"So, when are you coming to visit?"

"Soon, I promise."

Rain was on a high, not only was she satisfied with the outcome of the divorce; she was now free to marry the love of her life. Jerry was pleased upon hearing the news. It was exactly what he was waiting to hear. He and Rain had a lengthy conversation that night over dinner.

***

Across town

As he drove home later that night, he noticed a group of young women who had left a bar only seconds earlier. Two of the women were clutching beers with one hand while pulling on their skirts with their free hands. It was a wake-up call to the stranger who calmly observed them. They were young, urban professionals and upwardly mobile. Their behavior disturbed him. The two women said goodnight to their friends, walked to their car, and drove off. The stranger followed.

The women drove to Ninety-fourth Street and Central Park West. It was quiet. The stranger kept a close watch as they entered the building and out of his sight. He was about to drive off when he saw the shadow of a curvaceous figure by a second-floor window, seconds later, the lights came on. His hunch was right, as he smiled and drove off.

He returned two nights later and parked across from the park. He was bold. Someone was peeking through the blinds. He had a stoic look on his face as he crossed the street; never looking up at the image in the window. He was dressed like a delivery boy. A man was leaving the building, he entered, seconds before the door closed. He knew exactly where to go. Unbeknownst to the women, he had returned the next day and questioned a delivery boy, he saw leaving the building. He walked the one flight to the apartment and knocked on the door. He feared knocking it too loud. No one answered. He knocked it a bit harder.

"Who is it?" a voice said from behind the door.

"It's the delivery."

"The delivery? Joan, did you order food?" the woman asked her roommate, loud enough for him to hear.

"No . . ."

"Someone ordered food from this apartment. It's from Gloria's Restaurant. You guys always order from us," he responded.

"Yes, we do, but it could be one of the other tenants on the floor."

"You know what, I'll call and see if I have the right apartment."

"Okay," Joan said, opening the door. The stranger was stunned. He had goosebumps as the hair on his neck stood up. His only concern was whether the other tenants heard their conversation. Nonetheless, he wasn't going to let this prevent him from the task at hand. No sooner than the door was opened, he pushed his way inside and slammed the door behind him.

"Scream and you are both dead," he said to the women.

"Please don't hurt us."

"Shut the fuck up!" he barked. Tying them up, he forced a piece of cloth into their mouths, preventing them from speaking or crying out. He then began ranting and raving. They were terrified. "I have had my eyes on you for the past few days. You have been bad. You shouldn't drink and drive."

The women stared at each other trying to grasp what he was talking about. As he continued ranting, a look of confusion was on their faces.

They didn't know what to make of the things he was saying. He turned his back to them and then suddenly turned around and stood in front of Joan.

"If you even whisper too loud, I will snap your neck," he said, removing the cloth from her mouth. She nodded in agreement and exhaled.

"Why are you doing this to us?"

"No, you did it to yourself, you and her. Answer this for me, why were you drinking and driving?"

"We weren't drinking and driving."

"Yes. You were, I saw you. Don't lie to me!"

"I'm not lying. When was this?"

"Saturday night. You were with friends drinking and you two drove off with drinks in your hands. Don't you know it's against the law and you could have injured or killed others?"

"We are sorry. I'm sorry. We won't do it again, I promise."

"I don't think you'll have another chance to do so."

"What do you mean?" He didn't respond. He stuffed the cloth back in her mouth.

"You are careless, unreasonable, and inconsiderate and have no respect for the law; and for that, you must pay."

The women were flailing and sobbing as they awaited the inevitable. He reached into his pocket and put on a pair of gloves. He sat the women down facing one another. In his mind, one would see the other take her last breath. He approached Joan with the chloroform and placed it over her nose as her friend watched, horrified. With icy eyes and a solemn look on his face, he coldly stared at the friend.

As Joan's breath left her body, he smiled. He turned towards the friend, tightly cupped her chin, and stared into her eyes. He whispered in her ear, "It's your turn."

He calmly placed his hands around her neck and strangled her. He untied the bodies, removed the clothing, and laid them on the floor. He smiled, admiring his work. He cleaned up and closed the door behind him.

***

There was a huge police presence in front of the building and the surrounding blocks, which were cordoned off. The tenants were horrified at the murder of the two women and at how easily he got inside the building. They knew the Westside Killer had struck once again, and this hit close to home. The police were looking at all possibilities as they investigated the crime scene. They left nothing to chance. They followed up on every lead. They were adamant about letting anything hinder the investigation. There was a killer loose, stalking the community.

The police were well aware of the need to dispel the rumors of more than one serial killer. They feared if it were repeated enough, it could be established as a fact. Misinformation, opinions, and not curtailing the untruths oftentimes will brandish the department as not being proactive enough and thus not providing the necessary resources to apprehend the killer.

The investigators were convinced that it was a lone individual responsible for the killings and that he wasn't some kind of a dysfunctional loner. Chances are he's from the New York City area and knows his way around the city; and an ordinary guy who works, has a nice home and family, and lives in plain sight in the community and not some rural town. He was in his comfort zone.

One thing that stood out and which the investigators agreed on was that sex wasn't a motivational factor. The killer never sexually assaulted any of the victims; and they were certain that thrill-seeking, power, anger, and financial worth were some of the other factors, and they all had dark hair. The police were worried that other circumstances may also keep the killer busy and off their radar, which would be a major setback in getting him off the streets.

EPISODE

31

It was difficult for her not to think about those earlier days, after years of trying to forget. The emotions and the flashbacks wouldn't allow her to do so. Time was on her side. She had done the unthinkable she thought to herself. Her life had changed quite a bit. She had a wonderful group of friends; a mother and a sister who she loved dearly. Additionally, she had a mature, respectful, caring, and loving man. She never thought that she would meet a man like Jerry, after her failed marriage.

Yet it wasn't so long ago that she dreamt of spending the rest of her life with Jonathan Banks. Their eyes met one afternoon as she and a group of friends were jogging at the park. He was watching her from a distance. He was smitten by her beautiful face and smile. He returned her smile. She thought he was cute. She had the jitters as he approached the group. Her friends were smiling.

I'm so nervous and why is he coming over here? I hope he doesn't say anything to me, she said to herself.

He had a broad smile on his face, as she and her friends kept walking. Her tight-fitting, full-length spandex left nothing to the imagination. She jogged with the poise and elegance of a sexual panther, exuding an odor of arousing sexual desire. His eyes were focused on her slim frame and shapely ass as it jiggled with her every movement.

"Hello."

"Hi," she replied, trying not to display any emotions that would give the impression that she liked what she saw.

His eyes glowed, demanding her attention. Neither of them could resist the temptation and emotions that stirred inside. She was speechless for a moment.

"I'm Jonathan. Are you from around here?" He was under her spell, and it was written all over his face.

"I'm Rain, and no, I'm not."

"Can I have a word with you?"

"You are," she laughed.

"Yeah, you are right."

It wasn't a chance encounter by any stretch of the imagination. Jonathan believed the stars had aligned in his favor and it was inevitable that they would meet. In his mind, it was destiny, and as time went on, the two stayed in contact and soon became fast friends. Rain smiled as she reflected on the good times they shared. Over time, she learned that the things you can change, you ought to; and those you can't, you move on from.

This was a fresh start and one which she had some ambiguity about. Not that she was afraid of the direction in which her life was heading, but she questioned whether she was prepared. She knew all too well, how deceptive, secretive, and manipulative some people can be until they live together. Unlike what transpired between her and Jonathan, this wasn't the case with Jerry. She never lost faith in the fact that there are still a lot of down-to-earth people who are trustworthy, fair, and kind. She didn't want to leave any room for error, as she grasped the severity of what her life will be like in a few months or years.

***

He stood patting his feet as his father spoke. He had only arrived minutes earlier to inform him that he and Rain were going to get married. What happened next, he never expected, not in a million years.

"What do you know about this girl, son?"

"What do you mean by that? I know her."

"Are you sure? You don't just wake up and get married. You have to know everything about that person."

"What are you getting at, pops? What are you saying?"

"Are you sure you want to marry her?"

"Of course, I'm sure. What do you mean by if I want to marry her? You keep repeating yourself."

"Sit down, son."

"I don't want to sit down. I'm fine. Lay it on me. I'm ready."

"I think you should sit down."

"Okay, but if it's your money that you are worried about, she's not the gold-digging, money-grubbing type. Matter of fact, she's financially stable. She doesn't need your money. Her divorce came through and she came out of it pretty well. If it will make you feel any better, we are going to sign a pre-nuptial agreement. So, like I said pops, you don't have to worry about anything. If anything, I expected to get your blessings by coming here, not to hear this nonsense. Mother has already given me hers."

"Son, none of what you said is the reason for what I'm about to tell you."

"So, what is it then?"

"Remember a while back I told you I ran into a homeless girl at a local eatery, and I gave her some money for a meal?"

"Vaguely, but I'm listening."

"Well, it was her."

He had a shocked look on his face. He couldn't believe what he was hearing. He stared at his father. "Pops are you serious? Are you sure? You're saying that it was her? Rain?"

"Yes, I'm saying that. It's her. I remember her. I wouldn't lie to you. Why?"

"But if that's the case, don't you think she would have remembered you as well? Why would she come around, knowing that you were the one who gave her the money? It just doesn't make any sense, nor does it add up."

"Perhaps she doesn't recall, it happens, she was in a terrible situation."

Jerry paused. He stood up. A scowl was on his face, it was contorted. It was an expression of disappointment and pain. He was speechless. Yet he knew all too well that there are two sides to every story and that reaffirmed his conviction as his father spoke.

"The answer to your problem is a simple one."

"What do you mean by simple?"

"Just think about it."

"Think about what?"

"I don't know what to say or do."

"Since you don't know what to do, I'll tell you what you won't do."

"What's that?"

"You can't marry her. It won't look good."

"What? What do you mean I can't marry her?"

"You are not going to disgrace this family. I worked too mutha-fucking hard, and too long for my family to be looked upon with such disdain . . ."

Cutting him off, Jerry responded, "Disdain? Disdain from whom, what, and where? Are you talking about the tight-ass, ass-licking family members and so-called friends and associates of yours?"

"Don't you say such things? I built this mutha-fucka, me, I did!"

"Yes, you did, but I'm the one marrying her, not you. She makes me happy, and I love her. You expect me to believe your bullshit story and not question it?"

"Our family's legacy will be on the line if you marry that girl."

"So, Rain is going to destroy our family and everything else that orbits around your business and life, Oh Great One, is that it?"

"You better get some sense boy. This is not a game."

"You talk about legacy, what legacy? Look how you treated mother. You put her through a lot. She wasn't treated nicely by you, Oh Great One."

"Do not patronize me with your sarcastic remarks!"

"Don't flatter yourself. You were the cause of all her hurt and pain, and now you are acting as if you're so special. What role are you playing now, pops, the Equalizer? Denzel Washington already played that role."

"You think this is a damn game?"

"No, I don't, this is my life, and I could care less about some damn legacy. I can build my legacy. I have my own money. I don't need yours. I worked just as hard for mine as you did for yours. I had to work for it.

I wasn't handed a silver spoon. You know that. You made me work for it and I appreciated it, but I'm not going to let you dictate how I live my life based on some legacy. So, damn a legacy. You will not stop me from marrying her, by using your money, power, and wealth to change my mind. None of it will stop me from marrying the woman I love."

"Well then, I will have no other alternative but to remove you from my will if you do this. Don't be a damn fool. Think about what you are doing. There are lots of other women out there who are just as beautiful. It's not like you'll be downsizing, in all honesty, you'll be upgrading. Why can't you understand what I'm saying?"

"This is bullshit! I don't give a fuck about you and your will. But I'll be damned if I let you ruin my life. Why do you want to ruin my life?"

"I'm not doing anything to your life. You will be doing it to yourself if you marry that girl; you will have no one to blame but yourself."

"You know what pops?"

"What?"

"Fuck you!"

"How dare you talk to me in such a manner?"

"I'm sorry. I apologize. Go fuck yourself," he snapped, storming out of his apartment.

***

He was angry as he drove the short distance to Rain's apartment. The thought of calling her never crossed his mind. Within minutes he arrived.

"It's me, buzz me in," he said, as the buzzer sounded.

"Hi," Rain spoke, opening the door.

"Hey, thought I'd drop by; there's something I want to ask you."

"Sure, what is it?"

"It's about my father."

"Your father? What does your father have to do with me?"

"Sit down."

"Okay."

"He said you guys met before I introduced you."

"What? No way. I had never met your father until we were introduced."

"He said something different."

"What did he say?"

"He said you guys met at an eatery on the Lower East Side. You were homeless and he gave you some money."

She had a shocked look on her face. "Oh, my God! Oh, my God!"

"Is he telling the truth?"

Ashamed, she answered, "Yes. I didn't know that was your father. I'm so sorry. This was years ago. I had not too long arrived in the city, and I was doing terrible." She began sobbing. "You don't have to say anything else. I will leave you alone. I have embarrassed you and your family. I guess you came here to break the news to me, that you're leaving me, huh? You don't have to; I will do so on my own."

"You need to stop with the nonsense. I love you. I told him that I'm going to marry you no matter what."

"He told you not to marry me? Please, Jerry, I don't want to come between you and your family. Perhaps your father is right, maybe you shouldn't marry me."

"No, I'm going to marry you. But why didn't you tell me about the encounter?"

"I didn't know it was him. He looks different. I would have told you. Believe me, I would have. I'm so sorry."

"It's okay, it's behind you now. Nothing will prevent us from getting married."

"I don't think I could ever face your family again. It's too embarrassing."

"Stop talking like that."

"But what if he mentioned it to the rest of the family?"

"I don't think he did."

"Why do you think that?"

"I would have heard about it a long time ago."

"But I feel so dirty and ashamed."

"You shouldn't feel that way, things happen. I get it. You mean the world to me. Honestly, I don't think I could ever live my life without you being a part of it. I love you Rain, and I want you to be my wife."

"I love you too, Jerry. I do." She trembled as they embraced and kissed.

EPISODE

32

Although Ashley's stay with Rain wasn't long, the two stayed in contact. They refused to let anything break up their friendship, not even Ashley's relationship with Matthew. The two women had discussed Matthew on many occasions. He was smitten by Ashley's beauty, and he brought it to Rain's attention. She didn't mind, but she did explain to him that she was a nice girl and that she was looking for someone to love her and not play games with her. He assured her that he was through playing games, and Rain believed him. Knowing this, she felt comfortable as she sat down with Ashley. Ashley was a bit worried and felt uncomfortable talking about Matthew. But Rain reassured her that it was fine; that said, she gave them her blessings. Rain was somewhat relieved that he was in a relationship and would no longer be an annoyance to her and Kelly. She smiled at the thought.

Rain, Kelly, and Tatyana were having cocktails at Ashley's apartment when she informed them that she had some good news. The women were eager to hear what she had to say.

"Guess what?"

"What?" they asked.

"Matt and I are thinking about moving in together."

"You are?" the women were stunned, this they never expected and so soon.

"You guys must be in love, huh?" Kelly asked.

"Yeah."

"Congrats," Rain and Tatyana said.

"Thanks."

"I hope you know what you're doing," Tatyana added.

"I am. I love him."

"She loves herself some Matthew," Rain joked.

"It's written all over her face," Kelly joined in.

"I'm ready, but at the same time I'm kind of worried."

"Worried about what?" Rain asked.

"You know, living with a man. I don't know if I can do it."

"Of course, you can do it. Being worried is normal. It comes with the territory. You have to give it a try — if you don't, you will never know."

"I guess you're right. He's ready and I'm ready, so why not, right?"

"Girl, you will be fine. You have all our support."

"Thanks, guys."

Tatyana and Kelly didn't say much to one another. Their sexual romp was just that, a romp. There was still some tension between the two although they would never admit it. Rain picked up on it immediately and expressed her feelings to them before leaving. The women were reluctant to admit to each other that there was some tension. They held special memories for each other. What they had was special. It was a different time, and their innocence was their way of expressing themselves. They were infatuated with each other, but more importantly, it was guided by trust and love, which they felt would last longer than the outcome.

***

Days later

It was an immaculate house on the outskirts of Sagaponack, New York. An English country-style estate, the sprawling home includes eight en suite bedrooms, a 60-ft. heated pool, a tennis court, and a six-car garage. Included on the property are a pool house, an antique barn, and a carriage barn with a three-bay garage. The car came to a crawl as it pulled into the paved driveway. Ruth Benjamin emerged from the rear seat of the chauffeur-driven car. She made her way to the front door where she was greeted warmly by the butler.

"Tell him I'm here," she said.

"Hi Ruth, and how are you?" he said, greeting her.

"I'm fine, but there are some things that I need to talk to you about."

"Is it about what transpired at the apartment?"

"Yes."

"Come." They walked to his study.

"What happened between you and your son?"

"I only had a conversation with him. I was only telling him what the family expects of him."

"Are you sure about that?"

"What do you mean?"

"Perhaps it's your expectation and what you want of him."

"Come on now, Ruth."

"Herbert, it's his life. He's a grown man. How dare you tell him how to live his life? You were wrong for saying the things you did."

"She's not one of us."

"What do you mean? How dare you say that? She's someone's child. How foolish can you be? She's a very nice girl."

"It doesn't matter, as far as I'm concerned, she's an outsider, trash."

"How dare you call her that? You take that back this very minute, Herbert Benjamin."

"Fine, but I'm still not giving him my blessing."

"You are something else, do you know that? You told your son you will leave him out of your will if he marries the woman he loves? What is wrong with you? What are you thinking? I thought you were a rational and thoughtful man, but I'm convinced more than ever that you are not. Where did the Herbert that I have known all these years go? Huh, where is he? Is he becoming a bitter old man?" He never responded. "Say something. He worships the very ground that you walk on. He's been looking up to you his whole life. He's your son. He loves that girl. I'm warning you Herbert if you say a word to anyone about Rain's past you will regret the day you ever met me. And for your information, they are getting married, and you are invited. You're his best man. You think about that. Benjamin, he wants your blessings." She turned and walked away. He called out to her, but she ignored him. She was quickly ushered into the car and drove off.

**

Immediately after leaving Herbert's residence, Ruth called Jerry and told him about her conversation with his father. He wasn't pleased, to say the least, but what could he have said to his mother? He told her that he was going to marry Rain regardless of what his father said. His mother agreed. Later that night, Jerry told Rain what his mother said. She listened. She said she would support whatever decision he makes.

EPISODE

33

In the short time that Matthew and Ashley have known each other, their friendship grew beyond their expectations. Matthew's obsession with Rain and how their relationship ended was now a thing of the past. He fell head over heels in love with Ashley. He knew he wasn't going to allow her to leave after they were introduced, without saying a word. She wasn't so sure initially, but his persistence would eventually pay off. She finally gave in, and they went out on a date; it went well, and it took off from there.

Rain questioned Matthew's motives for pursuing Ashley as he did. He was disappointed in her for doing so, but he understood because they were friends.

"The last time we spoke about her, you promised that you wouldn't hurt her, and I hope you keep your word. Can you do that for me?"

"Hurt her? I wouldn't do that to her. Come on now."

"You said the same thing to me when we dated, remember?"

"Of course, I do, but this is different, I've grown since then. I know what I should or shouldn't do and hurting her isn't one of them."

"Are you sure about that?"

"Yes, I'm sure."

"Do you love her?"

"Rain, what the fuck is this, huh?" Am I being arrested?"

"You know that's not necessary."

"So, what's up with the questions? I don't know what to make of this."

"Do you?"

"Yeah, I do. Why the damn questions?" He was pissed.

"You know why I told you this before, she's my friend and I'm not going to stand by and watch her get hurt by you or anyone else."

"You know what?"

"What?"

"You and I dated. You and I both know a few things about each other, and I'm quite sure if there's one thing you know about me, it's that I fall in love easily. I wear my heart on my sleeve. See, I can say shit like this to you and it doesn't bother me. I love, Ashley. We love each other, and I know it might look bad, being that you guys are friends, and you and I dated, and people might start saying shit. . ."

Cutting him off, she said, "No, I have no problem with you guys dating or whatever people might say, shit like that doesn't bother me. It's whatever."

"Whatever, Rain?"

"Matt, you know I didn't mean that. I want you to be there for her because she's been through a lot like me."

"Yeah, I know. She told me, and this is why I'm not going to put her through any bullshit."

"Okay, I wish you two the best and I mean it."

"Thanks, who would have thought it?"

"Thought what?"

"That I would be going out with a white girl who is friends with my ex, and she's from out of state."

"You better stop while you're ahead." They laughed aloud as they hugged each other.

Matthew and Ashley moved in together as planned. Tatyana who was spending a lot more time in the city and by now was living with Rain had her eyes on Jordan. It didn't matter to Jordan that she and Rain were sisters. Left up to him, he would have slept with all the women in her family.

***

On March 18th, 2008, the Westside Killer struck again. He had been lying low for some time and his return shocked the city once again. Most New Yorkers knew he hadn't been caught and his reappearance opened old wounds.

He pulled into the parking spot at 12:30 am that morning. There he would randomly choose his victim. The reception had just ended. A group of mostly young women walked into the parking area, behind Charlottes Caterer off-Broadway and Seventy-Second Street. They got in their cars and drove off. He decided to follow a young brunette. She drove at a moderate speed before pulling up on Sixty-Seven Street and Central Park West. It was his old stomping ground. It seemed as if he was deliberately teasing law enforcement officials. She parked her car and began walking to her building. He parked not too far from her.

He hurried his steps, making sure not to bring any attention to himself. No sooner than she opened the door to the entrance of the building, he grabbed her from behind. He forced her to a section of the building where there weren't any cameras. Told to remain quiet, he forced her onto the elevator. Worried about the camera on the elevator, he hung his head low and held her close; giving the impression they were a couple. What he didn't know was that the camera wasn't working.

Once inside the apartment, he removed his disguise. But instead of tying her up and taping her mouth, he showed her several pictures of his victims. She was horrified. She stood there in shock. This was totally out of character.

He stared at her inconspicuously and strangely. His mind was elsewhere. He told her to remove her clothes. She had a blank stare on her face. She was about to speak when he said in an unassuming voice, "I told you not to say a fucking word. Now remove your fucking clothes before you end up like the others." She did as she was told. "Now come here."

Naked, she trembled in fear. He told her to sit.

"Do you know who I am?"

"Yes."

"So, tell me, who am I?"

"Please don't make me do this, please."

"Why not? Don't you want to know me?"

"Yes, I do, but I'd prefer not to say."

"Say it!" he snapped.

"The Westside Serial Killer."

"Do you think it's who I am? Do I look like a killer to you? Do I? Do you think I'm emotionally and psychologically unstable?" She was baffled. She didn't respond. "Answer me!" he snarled.

"No."

"Are you sure? Are you saying it to make me feel good?"

"No, it's the truth. You're not unstable just a bit . . ."

"A bit what, bizarre, weird, crazy, a nut, what?"

"No, no, you are none of the above," she said, glaring wide-eyed.

"What's your occupation?"

"They're on my bookshelf, the books, that's what I do."

"Who would have thought it? Did you ever think that you would come face to face with the Westside Serial Killer? I bet you didn't."

"No, I did not," she barely whispered.

"Ah, a psychologist, no wonder you said I wasn't unstable. Why? Because you would love to sit me down and discuss what makes me tick, don't you? It's okay, you don't have to lie."

"I'm home. I do not take my work home with me."

"You don't? I bet you do."

"I do not. What's your name?"

"You already know it. You said it a few minutes ago. Let's play a game."

"Please, I'm begging you."

"Would it surprise you if I were to get up and walk out of your apartment?"

"I'm begging you."

"Answer the fucking question, you're a psychologist."

"It would," she responded.

"And why is that?"

"Because I saw your . . ."

He interrupted her. "Lay down." She complied.

He gagged her mouth. He held her arms above her head and slowly began tying them. She stared at him with pleading eyes, begging as tears welled up in them. It seemed by design as the tears slowly rolled down her cheeks. Her impenetrable hazel eyes, now a shell of its former self were empty. It was lifeless. He had strangled her. He removes the gag and unties her. As is customary, he cleaned up after himself and left her naked body on the floor.

EPISODE
34

Kelly was upset that Blair hadn't followed Matthew's lead. Like Matthew, she thought he would come to his senses and did likewise. She made it known that he and Ashley hadn't known each other long. Yet the love they had for each other mattered and was the reason for them moving in together. Blair tried to explain his reason for them waiting once again, but it was to no avail. Kelly would have none of it. Somehow, he managed to convince her that their circumstances differed and after some time she calmed down.

Blair had his doubts about Matthew and Jordan. He thought Matthew was always looking for a handout, a moocher so to speak. Although employed, he was correct in his assessment; Matthew pursued mostly gainful working, educated, and professional women. Financially independent women were his ideal choice and he pursued them vigorously.

Jordan, he thought was superficial, a player, and a big phony. He would do almost anything to gain an advantage over his friends, while behind their backs trying to seduce their women. He wasn't the type to hide his feelings and how he truly felt. Although Blair was friends with both men, he had a much closer relationship with Matthew. Unlike Jordan, who berated him at every opportunity and to anyone who would listen, Matthew never said anything derogatory about him.

Jordan and Rain's friendship had strained some, it wasn't Rain's undoing but rather his. It had become unbearable for Rain, who was tired of his impromptu rants whenever Kelly and Blair would accompany them to their book signings. The two discussed the matter, but as usual, Jordan was unreasonable. It didn't help any, though he was dating Tatyana. Rain hadn't come to terms with the idea of them dating. They were far from the ideal couple because he continued his womanizing ways. Rain warned her about him, but she responded that she would be fine and that he wasn't as smart as her, to which the women laughed.

Kelly wasn't as forthcoming with their relationship either and she brought it to Tatyana's attention. What worried her was Jordan knowing about their past relationship. But Tatyana's answer was always no. It was a foregone conclusion and although he did pry, he never got anywhere. Moreover, Rain's wedding was upcoming and neither one of them needed the distraction.

***

Rain was doing well, her last two novels made the Literature Best Sellers List, along with Jordan's. He also made the Tabloid Writers Best Sellers List. Things were looking promising, and he was feeling good about himself, not that he wasn't. Yet he still harbored some resentment towards Rain and Jerry. He hated the fact that she never gave him a chance. Moreover, he felt that he was a better suitor than Jerry and wondered what she saw in him other than his money. He was still pissed that he was rebuffed by his cousin. Despite how he felt, he never missed the chance to attend the many affairs the two invited him to.

The tension between him and Matthew never ceased. There were the occasional stares, but that's as far as it went. Blair didn't fear any better as far as Jordan was concerned. He spoke badly about him behind his back. His problem with Blair was that he came out of nowhere and immediately became a part of the group. He made it clear to Kelly and Rain on numerous occasions, but they would tell him that he was paranoid.

***

He was sitting in his car across from Rain's apartment building when she noticed the car. Initially, she wasn't going to approach him, but she couldn't resist the temptation. She was angry. He saw her as she approached.

"What are you doing here?"

"I'm waiting for your sister."

"Oh, you've been waiting long?" just then Tatyana exited the building.

"Hi, sis?" Tatyana called to her. "Where are you coming from?"

"Jerry's place."

"Oh, I'll be back later tonight. I'll call you."

"Okay."

Rain had an unpleased look on her face. She was upset that Jordan knew where she lived. That night when Tatyana returned, she admonished her about it. Her excuse was that Rain should have told her. According to her, she wasn't a mind reader. Rain eventually overlooked the matter. Her wedding date was set, and preparations were being made; and although Jordan was a pain in the ass, now was not the time to deal with him.

Rain was one lucky woman. She was excited when Jerry proposed to her. She remembered it as if it were yesterday. She screamed in excitement when she saw the ring he placed on her finger. She smiled to herself. She saw to it that Kelly, Tatyana, and Ashley were a part of the bridesmaid assembly along with Jerry's two nieces.

**

Ashley had become suspicious of Blair whom she felt had crossed her invisible line. His behavior was troubling. The two spoke at several of the private affairs they were invited to by Rain and Jerry. She thought he was coming onto her, and it bothered her greatly. On one occasion, he questioned her as to whether she loved Matthew. Shocked at the question, she told him how rude and obnoxious he was. Nonetheless, it didn't stop him from making his usual remarks and comments. She thought about bringing it to Kelly's attention but decided not to after thinking it through. As the newcomer to the group, she didn't want to ruffle anybody's feathers. With that in mind, she went about things as normally as possible.

"Don't pay any attention to him. I've had my eyes on him," Matthew told her.

"I don't like how he stares at me."

"Hmm. I know he likes you. I can tell."

"That's crazy; he's got, Kelly. What is wrong with him?"

"Babes, some men are like that," he said, "they're never satisfied."

"Believe me I know."

"He stares at me all the time at work, but I pretend as if I don't see it."

"He does?"

"Yeah, I'm used to him."

"Do you say much to each other?"

"Yeah, we do. But like I said, I'm not worried about him. I'll step to him if it gets to that."

"I don't want it to get physical between you and him."

"I understand. Even though he stares at you, I'll give him the benefit of the doubt because I know he's crazy in love with Kelly."

"But still, it's creepy to me and I hate it."

"I'll have a word with him tomorrow at work."

"Baby, I don't know if it's a good idea. Are you sure you want to do that?"

"Yeah, I'm sure. It will be alright."

The next day

"Hey, Blair, can I have a word with you?"

"Sure. What is it?"

"It's about, Ashley."

"Okay, what about her?"

"She seems to get uneasy when you're around and the way how you look at her."

"She does? Hey, man, I'm sorry if she feels like that. I wasn't trying to disrespect either of you and if I came off that way; I'm sorry and I apologize."

"I understand. I just thought I'd bring it to your attention."

"No, no, no, you did the right thing. I would have done the same, and I sincerely apologize. No hard feelings?" he extended his hand.

"None," he said, shaking it.

***

Getting out of his car, Blair took several long strides as he made his way to Kelly's apartment building. Although he had apologized to Matthew, it bothered him that Ashley felt the way she did. It wasn't as if she was lying. Once inside the apartment, he began telling Kelly about the conversation he had with Matthew. He had a disturbed look on his face as he spoke. Kelly listened. She demanded to know if he had done what Ashley accused him of. He explained to her that they spoke, but it was innocent and nothing more.

That night she sat in bed questioning their relationship. She knew that he loved her and that he could have remained silent and not mentioned the conversation. *Maybe he should have kept it to himself,* she thought. Eventually, she would have heard it from Matthew, but would she have taken it lightly and ignored it, or would she have approached the two? They were faithful to each other and expected nothing less. They continued their torrid affair, nonetheless. Kelly never discussed the matter with Matthew and neither did he.

***

Days before the bridesmaid's final rehearsal, Kelly and Rain discussed at length how she and Jerry were dealing with the excitement surrounding the wedding; notwithstanding, she and Kelly had a lot of catching up to do and they never found the time to do so. So, to finally sit down and talk, was something they both wanted to do.

"We have been friends ever since I arrived here in New York, and you have been a wonderful friend. I remember the first time I saw you; I was like who is the hot chick with the shapely figure, looking like she's all that," Rain said to her.

"I thought the same thing when I saw you and a bit more."

"I know you did," both women laughed.

"But you know what, Rain?"

"What?"

"You have not only been a great friend, but you have also been a sister to me. You were what I needed when we met; a strong woman who could inspire me. We both experienced a lot, but we never gave up. We knew there were still some good men left and you have found yours and I am so happy for you. Words cannot describe how happy I am; and despite the times when we disagreed, I always knew that I wasn't going to let a friendship like ours end for no reason at all. I love you my sister and I wish you and Jerry a lifetime of joy, happiness, and laughter. I love you, Rain."

"Oh, my God! You are making me cry. I love you too, Kelly. Our friendship is a lasting one and I am so glad I came to New York because I met you, and no matter where Jerry and I end up in life; you will always be in my heart and my thoughts. I love you."

EPISODE

35

It was an old building from World War 1, located near the corner of Seventy-Fifth Street. Most of the tenants had lived there for years. Legend has it that several of the early Hollywood movie stars lived there before becoming famous. For years, the list to move into the building grew as did the rent.

He waited several feet from the building. It was dark out. It was what some would refer to as midnight darkness. He quickly began observing a small group of women who were walking to the building. He took several steps and decided that it wasn't such a good idea. He didn't want to take the chance with so many of them. Also, he had to be mindful of the plain clothes and uniformed officers who were on patrol. He waited. It wasn't long before he saw the young woman who would become his next victim.

She was with her daughter, who looked about five years old. She had a small stuffed giraffe in her hand. She saw the figure standing not too far from the building. Handing her daughter her cell phone, she fumbled for her keys. He pretended as if he was on the phone. She didn't make much of it. She held her daughter tightly and approached the entrance to the building. His strides were meticulous and deliberate. He laughed loud enough for her to hear. She noticed that his face was partially hidden. A cool crisp breeze blew. As she opened the door, he said thank you and entered the lobby of the building, all the time laughing and talking on the phone.

She was nervous, but it wasn't enough for her to consider screaming or running. She prayed that he was just another tenant. They made their way inside the elevator and there she got a good glimpse of his face. He smiled. She did likewise. He seemed rather pleasant she thought. What she didn't notice was that he never pressed any of the buttons. The elevator came to a stop on the seventh floor. She held her daughter's hand and said goodnight before exiting the elevator. She made her way down the quiet hallway. Her apartment was the second one to her left. She fumbled with the keys before opening the door. The giraffe fell from the little girl's hand.

She never saw what hit her and when she turned around it was too late. In a flash, he shoved her, the little girl, and the giraffe inside the apartment and closed the door behind them.

"Is there anyone else in here?" he asked.

"No," she said, sobbing softly.

"Take her and put her to bed and if she screams, I will snap her little neck." She did as he said.

He followed her and watched as she put her to sleep, laying her giraffe next to the pillow. Within minutes, she was fast asleep. He barricaded the bedroom with the living room couch. He then tied up the mother. He failed to see that the mother put her cell phone under the giraffe

"What is it that you want?"

"You."

"Me?"

"Yes."

"Why? What did I do?"

"It doesn't matter."

"If it's money you want, you can have it."

"Money? I don't want your money."

"Then what is it that you want?"

"Your life," he said, as he pounced on her in one motion, gagging her mouth. She was at his mercy.

"Why do you women think you are so fucking smart, huh?" She stared at him with wide eyes. "Every single one of you thinks and acts the same. But you know what? I know you." He stared down at her.

She watched him as he looked over the apartment. Taking a seat, he began his tirade once again. "I have known women like you for most of my life and every one of you has deceived, rejected, and discarded me as if I'm garbage." She could only whimper. "You left me alone. You cast me aside. You deserted me. But you know what? I made something of myself, and you didn't."

He got up and soaked the gag with the colorless sweet-smelling liquid chloroform. Minutes later, it was over. He smiled. He removed her clothes and placed her in the usual position. He cleaned up like he always does. What he didn't know was that the little girl had watched the whole thing unfold. Using her tiny frame to slightly push the door ajar, she used her mother's cell phone to snap his photo.

She ran back into the bed as his footsteps got closer. She cowered as he pushed the couch aside and opened the door. He had a cloth filled with chloroform. He stared at her tiny frame for several seconds. He wrestled with his thoughts. He paced back and forth before leaving the room. Looking over his artistry once again, he closed the door behind him and got on the elevator.

EPISODE

36

Rain and Jerry were married on the Benjamin's estate in upstate New York, in a private ceremony. The newlyweds spent their honeymoon in St. Barts, a chic and upscale island in the Caribbean, a favorite of the rich and famous. After their honeymoon, they moved into the luxurious One 57 building in Midtown Manhattan and bought a summer home on the south coast of Maine. Yet what took place leading up to the wedding and during the ceremony was something no one could have foreseen.

Although their rush to the altar wasn't an expeditious one, for some, including Jerry's father, it seemed so. He didn't believe they were in love, and no matter how much they tried to convince him; he was unyielding. He made it clear that he would not attend the wedding. Jerry was visibly upset on the day of the wedding. He wanted his hero, his father to be the best man. Instead, he had to replace him with a cousin of his.

Rain was beautiful as she stood next to her man. Their eyes sparkled with love. She wore an Italian silk voile corseted sheer sheet gown. With ecru palette with accents of flesh tones and handmade silk with Swarovski crystals; the train was laced with accents of peacock feathers. The groom was dressed in a Kiton K-50 suit, from London's famed Saville Row.

Ruth and other family members hadn't given up on Herbert showing up. Yet they had their doubts. The Minister was about to speak when there were hushes and stares. It was Herbert, Jerry smiled half-heartedly. *At least he showed up,* he thought to himself. The bridesmaids and groomsmen looked on, surprised. Ruth smiled at Jerry. But instead of taking a seat, Herbert kept walking toward the couple and without saying a word, Jerry's cousin reached into his pocket and handed him the bride's ring. He smiled, embraced his son, and stood next to him. Both men were teary-eyed. Herbert had always been there for his son, and having him there, standing next to him, on his special day, and during this special moment, meant the world to Jerry. It was a bond and love, between father and son, that moved everyone. Ruth's eyes filled with tears as she waved at her son.

The couple exchanged their vows as Kelly, Tatyana, and Ashley smiled. The three, excited, hugged her. Father and son embraced once again, and at that moment, with his father standing next to him, Jerry asked everyone to remain seated. He looked into his father's eyes and said, "What I'm about to say to you means a lot to me, and how much you have meant to me." And if the eyes are truly the windows to one's soul, then on this day; and at that moment, it was on display. All eyes were on Jerry as they anticipated his every word. There was an uncanny silence. He began:

> *I watch every step this man takes.*
> *I listen to every sound this man makes.*
> *I feel every expression on this man's face, and*
> *I hold this man's body when we embrace.*
>
> *I want to cry every tear this man cries.*
> *I want to try every task this man tries.*
> *I want to keep every memory this man keeps.*
> *I want to leap every mountain this man leaps.*
>
> *I want to be like this courageous man.*
> *Because I love this man the best way I can.*
> *I love you, Father. I want you to know.*
> *I want to be like you and walk in your shadow.*
>
> *I want to feel this man's pains.*
> *I want to be locked in this man's chains.*
> *I want to be his role model and live with his great name.*
> *For I am this man's son, and I'll never bear shame.*

Herbert Benjamin stood there speechless and teary-eyed. His legs almost gave out. He gasped for breath as he hugged his son. There were several outbursts of sobbing as Herbert and Rain hugged each other. It was a heartwarming scene; unlike anything the guests were prepared for.

It was an amazing night, to say the least. Ruth and Theresa laughed and chatted as if they had known each other all their lives. Their faces radiated with love for the newlyweds. The guests were having a wonderful time dancing and eating when Jordan sat down at Matthew and Ashley's table.

"It was beautiful wasn't it, guys? Wasn't she a beautiful bride?" Jordan said to Matthew and Ashley.

"Yes, it was," they both replied.

"I guess you guys will be doing it next, huh?"

Laughing, Ashley answered, "Perhaps in the foreseeable future, but not right now."

Jordan let out a hearty laugh. "You know what that means don't you, Matt?"

"I guess so."

"You better hurry and marry her before someone else sweeps her off her feet."

"You may be onto something."

"I know I am." Getting closer, he whispered in his ear. "If I were you, I would." He laughed before getting up and walking away.

"I guess he's had a bit too much to drink tonight."

"He looks like it," Ashley said, "he's a fucking jerk. I don't like him."

"Honey, forget about him."

"Okay, but I do want you to know that I will marry you one day."

"One day? It may be sooner than you think. But I wasn't going to say that to him." They laughed.

"Oh, here comes, Blair, I'm going to have a word with Kelly and the bride."

"Okay."

"Hi, Ashley," Blair said to her. She said hi and kept going.

A smiling Matthew, with his hands clasped, kept his eyes on Blair as he approached. "Hey, what's up bro? Nice, isn't it?" Blair said.

"It sure is. That was some heavy shit that Jerry said to his dad, wasn't it?"

"No doubt. I felt it."

"Yeah, sometimes you have to tell people how much you love them because you never know. His father has been his role model his whole life and that's what it's all about."

"I guess it needed to be said."

"Absolutely."

"That Jordan, isn't he something?"

"What do you mean?"

"The guy is supposedly seeing Tatyana, but he wants to know every woman in the damn place."

"Him and Tatyana, that shit is off and on; and to be honest with you most of the time it's off." The two laughed.

"But I thought he was a player?"

"He thinks he's one."

"I noticed him talking to you and Ashley. That guy is always talking," Blair said.

"He said some shit about if we're going to get married soon."

"See, that's the shit I'm talking about. He might be after your woman too. The dude is on a mission. So, you better watch out."

Matthew thought about bringing up the conversation they had about Ashley, but instead, he laughed and said, "This is one woman that he'll never get."

"There you go bro because I'm not giving up on the love of my life either. My brother, let me say this to you. I'm sorry about what happened, and I sincerely apologize to you and Ashley."

"It's cool. Hey, man, tonight is about our good friends Rain and Jerry."

"No doubt. But it doesn't bother you that your ex-girlfriend got married to a man that you know, and you're at the wedding?" Matthew had a dubious look on his face.

"No, it doesn't; maybe once upon a time, but not anymore. She's a lifelong friend."

"I hope you don't take it the wrong way. It wasn't intended to be taken that way."

"Oh, no! I understand bro. I would have asked the same thing if it was the other way around."

"No doubt. Man, you need to get up and go dance with that beautiful woman of yours."

"Yeah, you're right." No sooner than he left, Ashley returned.

"It's written all over your face, what did he say?" she asked.

"This fucking guy asked me how I felt being here and seeing my ex marrying another man."

"No, he didn't. Between him and that asshole Jordan, I don't know who is worse."

"I thought about kicking his ass right here . . ."

"Baby, no. He's an asshole. Don't go there with him."

"Yeah, you're right."

Rain and Jerry thanked their guests for taking time out of their busy schedules to share in their special moment and for that they were grateful.

EPISODE

37

The honeymoon was over, and Rain returned to work. She was greeted by her co-workers who threw her a party. While she was appreciative, she playfully chided them. Kelly was glad she returned. She had gotten fed up with Matthew and Blair. She complained to Rain that it was enough seeing Blair at work. Rain laughed.

"So, when are you guys going to move in? Didn't you say you had put it to him?"

"I did. But I don't think he's ready. Remember the concocted story I told you about?"

"Yeah, what about it?"

"It was concocted." The women laughed.

"I think he will come around."

"He better be sooner rather than later or else I'm going to give him his walking papers."

"You can't do that. That's not fair. You have to give him some time. Didn't you go through something like that? I did." The look on Kelly's face indicated that she didn't want to talk about her past at least not at that moment.

"Yeah, I guess you're right."

"Oh, since we are talking about this, didn't you say you had something to tell me about your past relationship?"

"I will."

"What is the big secret?"

"It's nothing."

"If it's nothing then why are you beating around the bush?"

"I'll tell you."

"Okay."

"But not right now."

"It better be some really serious shit; having me wait all this time."

"It's not that serious, but I promise it's good. It's just that I keep forgetting. Just remind me next time."

"I just did."

"I don't mean now, next time." They laughed.

***

The police were alarmed that the killer's latest victim was a young mother with a young daughter; and who may have seen her mother's killer. This certainly wasn't his way of doing things. Was he changing his modus operandi? Was it a mistake? Was he getting sloppy? The early responders were horrified when they came to the crime scene. The child was on her knees trying to wake her mother. An officer cradles her in his arms. He sees her stuffed giraffe; he reaches for it, and there lies the phone.

"Whose phone is this?" the officer asked her.

"My mommy," she answered, as he carried her out of the apartment and to an awaiting police car, where she was taken to relatives, and the female officers on the scene.

Smiling, the officer asked, "So what were you doing with it? Were you playing with it? I bet it was fun, huh? Wasn't it?"

She had the cutest smile on her face when she said, "No, my mommy gave it to me to hold when we got out of the car."

"So, you were playing with it the whole time?"

She shook her head, "Ah-ha. But my mommy took it back from me."

"She did?"

"Yeah. She put it under my giraffe when she was talking to the man in my room. I took his picture."

Shocked was an understatement as the officer handed the phone over to his superiors and told them what the girl said. They scrambled back to their headquarters and checked the phone. But to their dismay, it was only a partial side shot of his face. The photo was quickly enhanced but it still wasn't much to go on. But from the image and what the little girl said, they could tell that he was a black male. They had to be sure before saying anything to the press, which was quick to rush to judgment especially since the killer was black. The investigators felt if he was watching the nightly news and saw this; it might rattle him some, but to what extent only time will tell. The police had finally gotten a clue they felt would help in the investigation. What they weren't expecting was that it would come from a five-year-old.

One of the officers wanted to know why he couldn't empathize with his victim after seeing such a young child. His partner responded that he doubted that he had any room for empathy, but further went on to say that it's up to the forensic psychiatrists to figure it out. Their job is to get him off the street before he finds another victim.

When they finally disclosed the news, the media was abuzz. The city's newspapers displayed the grainy image and the captions read: Evil Comes in All Color! Serial Killer Strikes Again! The First Glimpse of a Killer!

***

The investigators were correct in their assessment in that the Westside Serial Killer didn't empathize with his victims and the lives they led. He was a serial killer, and he didn't show his victims any mercy. There weren't any motives for his brutal savagery. They knew he killed his victims by strangulation and the use of chloroform.

Most New Yorkers were stunned upon hearing the killer was a black male. They had accepted the narrative that serial killers were white. So, it came as a shock to those who subscribed to this belief. Several black and Latino men were placed under surveillance, accosted, and searched by members of the security forces. The city was on high alert. Police investigators feared that the killer would retaliate more so than ever because of the exposure and attention surrounding the case.

***

Rain was at home with Jerry watching the evening news when the image flashed across the screen. They studied the image carefully, but it didn't resemble anyone that they knew. Like most New Yorkers, they were prepared to call 1-800-577-TIPS.

"I hope they catch this guy soon," Rain said.

"Yeah, the police are trying to do their best. But I think they have a good lead. It might be a grainy photo, but someone might know who it is."

"I hope so. It was so sad that he would do such a horrific act in front of that little girl. He must be sick. I hope they catch his ass sooner rather than later."

"It's sickos like him we need to get off the street. But I'm somewhat surprised that he's black. What about you?"

"Yeah, I'm surprised also. I would have never thought it."

"The cops say he knows the neighborhood pretty well."

"These killings have been going on since I arrived in the city. When I lived in Brooklyn, they found a body or bodies I think, under the Williamsburg Bridge; it was his early victims."

"That's how serial killers operate at least some of them. It could go on for years. Remember that serial killer who killed and raped those thirteen women in California?"

"No, I knew about John Wayne Gacy, Dennis Rader, and the Zodiac Killer."

"This guy's name was Chester Turner. He, Ted Bundy, and the rest are all the same. You know they never caught the Zodiac Killer?"

"Yeah, I know. Baby, I don't want to talk about this anymore."

"Okay, so what now?" she smiled.

EPISODE

38

He was angry; she was in reasonable fear for her life. She didn't lead a high-risk lifestyle. But he was out of control, and she would be his next victim. Only twenty years old, she made the mistake of running by the pond in Central Park. One of his victim's bodies was found not too far from there. He caught up to her and dragged her into the bushes. She fought for her life, but he quickly overpowered her and strangled her. He removed her running pants and top and positioned her like he did his other victims.

The city was alarmed and upset that the police had allowed him to strike again. Central Park and the surrounding area were on high alert, and this worried the community. How could he have gotten past security? This troubled them deeply. Were their officers on duty at the time, or were they off? Did anyone hear her scream? These were some of the questions asked of the police by the community.

He was mocking the police and they knew it. They believed it would only be a matter of time before he made a mistake. They thought the image shown on television got him angry. The police stepped up their patrol and increased the task force. Overwhelmed with several unsubstantiated tips and suggestions by well-meaning citizens, the investigators were perplexed at the lack of substantial information.

Days later

He sat in front of the mirror and began reflecting. Now and then he mumbled to himself. It was plain as yesterday as he remembered the huge sycamore tree that held so many childhood memories. A massive tree, its branches hovered over the backyard like powerful arms.

'I used to press myself against that tree when we played hide-and-seek. I don't know who it was, but someone made a swing, and me and my friends would swing each other at every opportunity. I always wondered who climbed that big ole' tree and put up the swing. That tree gave our yard life. It did. People would flock to our home to see that big ole' tree, and that had a lasting effect on me. How so? Because it drew attention to itself without asking for it; it was powerful. It stood above all the other trees, and no one could chop it down. Power, that's what it was about. It was then that I decided to be like that tree. I was going to bring attention to myself and let everybody know who I was.'

'Is that what you think?'

'Yes. Look at them, how many has it been? One, two, three, I can't even count.'

'It wasn't you who did it. I did it.'

'You always want to take credit for the things that I do and that's not fair.'

'*Without me, you're nothing but a sorry pathetic, incompetent ass.*'

'*Don't you call me that?*'

'*Why shouldn't I?*'

'*Because you need me more than I do you.*'

'*Really? You fell for their bait.*'

'*What bait?*'

'*They wanted you to strike again and you did.*'

'*So, what was I supposed to do, sit back and let them have all the attention? No, I need the attention. It's not theirs. I gave them a job. They weren't doing a damn thing until I came on the scene.*'

'*And you believe this?*'

'*Yes. I am that big sycamore tree. I hover above them. They cannot outsmart me.*'

'*That was exactly what they wanted.*'

'*So, what now? I'm supposed to be afraid?*'

'*Shut up because I will have to save your stupid ass like I always do.*'

'*I told you not to talk to me like that.*'

'*Give me a break. I'm the intelligent one here, not you.*'

'*You might be but I'm the one who goes out night after night. You wanna know why?*'

'*Why, my intelligent friend?*'

'*Because I'm not afraid. You're the one that's afraid. When did you ever take the chance and go out? When? Never, that's the real reason. I dare you to do what I do.*'

'*There's no need for me to do anything when I have you.*'

'*Don't you think this is enough? We have been acting like fools.*'

'*You're right. We need to trust each other. What do you say?*'

'*I agree,*' he said to himself, getting up from the mirror.

***

Kelly was in a somber mood as she left work. She had a lot on her mind. She began questioning her friendship with Rain. Was she a good friend? She was starting to doubt it very much. Self-doubt was creeping in. She had lots to say, and Rain needed to hear it. Yet she thought everything would just go away. As she drove home, she began thinking about Blair and the promises he made to her. Were they mere lies? Competence, money, aspirations, motivation, and unparalleled conduct are among the most delightful effects of a first-class man's success; and this is what Kelly envisioned when she met, Blair. He epitomized these attributes and she wanted to support, love, and be there for him.

It had gotten to the point where Blair would approach Ashley at every opportunity wanting to talk. He would go to unimaginable lengths to get her attention. He would have numerous conversations with Jordan and Jerry, and it grew from there. Kelly was upset when she found out he visited Herbert's office. She wanted to know why.

According to him, they ran into each other at a local restaurant in mid-town Manhattan. It wasn't long before his visits to Herbert's office became more frequent. She was even more enraged when she found out that Janet worked with Herbert.

This bothered her and when she brought it to his attention, he denied any wrongdoings. She wasn't accusing him, but rather, why all of a sudden, he had become friendly with everybody; not to mention Jordan; who disliked him. Was their friendship more important than her? Had he been leading her on only to get close to Janet?

She had a lot on her mind as she drove, but instead of going home, she called Rain. No sooner than she arrived at Rain's apartment, she apologized. Rain accepted her apology.

"So, what is it that you have to tell me?"

"Something I should have told you a long time ago."

"So, what is it?"

"It's about, Jordan."

"Jordan? What about him?"

"He and I were in a relationship."

"Are you serious? You were?"

"Yup."

"Why didn't you tell me this earlier?"

"I wanted to, but I thought it would go away, and I thought it did, until the book party."

"The book party where we were introduced?"

"Yes. I never thought in a million years that you two would get so cool. And it bothered me."

"Wow! So how long did you two date?"

"It was long trust me. It was during the time I was going through a lot of shit."

"I see. Now it all makes sense."

"What makes sense?"

"You froze that night when you saw him."

"You're damn right I did."

"I saw it. It was written all over your face. He seemed surprised too."

"I bet he did."

"Really?"

"He's the one I was seeing when I was being stalked by Samantha. He was the boyfriend I moved in with."

"It was, Jordan? Wow!"

"Yup."

"Was he different back then?"

"He was. Nothing like this. He was everything any woman would want, not the conceited person he has become."

"I can't believe it. Was he writing back then?"

"No, he wasn't. He was working in insurance at the time. I was surprised when he told me that he was an author. He's a very intelligent guy, that much I can say. I wasn't aware, maybe it's because I don't read as much as I should."

"You and books? No, I don't see it." The two laughed. "That guy is something else. He had the nerve to try and talk to me. And Tatyana with her crazy ass is dating him off and on."

"He's a dog."

"Wasn't he a dog back then? Because a dog is a dog no matter how many owners he's had."

"When we were together it was just me and him. I know what I'm saying. He was a good man back then. I don't know what's wrong with Tatyana. She's upset at me for dating Blair, and she turns around and dates that egotistical selfish fool. I don't get it."

"She's my sister and I love her — but she's your ex." They laughed aloud. "The crazy thing is that he's still trying to talk to Janet."

"He is?"

"Yes, he is."

"He's a dog. Being that you mentioned Janet, Blair has been trying to talk to her."

"I know she works with Mr. Benjamin, and I found out that he has shown up a few times while she's there."

"Yes. He's been talking to her and Mr. Benjamin quite a lot."

"What the fuck? Is he trying to talk to her?"

"I don't know if he's trying to talk to her like that, but I don't like it."

"All I can tell you is to talk to him in-depth about it. As for Jordan, I'm going to let Jerry know that he's still trying as well."

"Okay, but I asked him about it. But he says it's innocent."

"I see. I'll ask Janet about it."

"Yes, do that. He's been talking to Jordan a lot too, and you know he doesn't like him. I've tried to explain this to him on numerous occasions, but he doesn't seem to get it."

"He's been doing the same thing at work with Matthew. You better check that man of yours. Do you know a new year is right around the corner? You can't start the new year like that."

"You are right, and I'm not."

"So, are you guys moving in together anytime soon?"

"He hasn't said much about it. But I'm not going to put up with it. He's got another thing coming if he thinks he's going to have his cake and eat it too."

"That's right, he needs to do something, but I'm still shocked that you and Jordan dated. Small world, isn't it?"

"It sure is, and I'm so sorry I took so long to tell you. Can you forgive me?"

"Of course, I'm just happy that we are friends and that our friendship has gotten stronger over the years."

"I was so happy for you on your wedding day, Mrs. Benjamin." They laughed. "You were a beautiful bride and I know Jerry will take care of you and treat you like the queen you are. You are my best friend, and I will always love and support you."

"Muah, muah, kisses! Hugs!" The women hugged and spent the rest of the evening talking and drinking.

The next day, Rain sat down with Tatyana. She warned her about Jordan and told her that he and Kelly dated. Tatyana was shocked, but after Rain explained everything, she promised that she wouldn't make a big deal about it. And that she would end the relationship. Rain was satisfied.

EPISODE

39

He waited by the building. It was only minutes earlier that she got off the train. She stopped at the local deli and then headed home. Seconds before she approached the building, he gained entrance from an unsuspecting tenant. He quickly noticed that there weren't any security cameras inside the building. He watched her from the staircase as she waited for the elevator. It was a six-story apartment building. He took the stairs, stalking her as the elevator came to a stop on the fourth floor. He was waiting. He pounced upon her and punched her in the face as she exited the elevator.

"Scream and I'll fucking kill you," he said to her, as she opened the door to her apartment.

"I won't," she replied, terrified. "It's . . ."

He quickly tied her up; blindfolded and gagged her. He stared at her. He was angry. He ripped her clothes off, exposing her nakedness.

"You're thinking, aren't you? You want to know who I am, right? And why I'm doing this, aren't you? Well, guess what? You don't know me. None of you know me." He sneered at her. "That's your man, huh?" He looked up at the photographs hanging on the wall and said they were a nice couple, but he would have made a much better choice. Her muffled sounds told him what she thought of his statement. He wanted to know what time the man in the picture would be home. He whispered in her ears, mocking her. She kicked and thrashed her body. Enraged, he had made up his mind to teach her a lesson. He taunted her as he waited. He removed the small container of chloroform from his inside jacket pocket and placed it on the table. Then he did something out of character, he pulled a .38 special from his waistband.

As the hours passed, he became more agitated. Suddenly, the sounds of keys caught his attention. Gun in hand, he positioned himself and waited. Not expecting an intruder in his home and without warning, the boyfriend was greeted by a loud thud, as he was bashed across the head. Dazed, and with blood streaming down his face, he fell to the floor. Within seconds, he was bound and gagged. When he finally came to, he was lying next to his girlfriend. His frantic eyes found the face of his attacker. He swallowed his saliva. Baffled, he stared at the killer's face, all the while trying to make sense of what was happening, and why. He desperately tried to move his body, as if to ask, why was he doing this to them?

The killer tortured them for hours before turning up the music. He removed the blindfold from the woman's eyes. The couple stared at each other knowing the inevitable. Teary-eyed, the woman watched as he put a pillow over her boyfriend's head and pulled the trigger. Turning to her, he pulled a rag from his back pants pocket and soaked it with chloroform. He put it over her nose and held it. Her body contorted and twisted as he snapped her neck. She fought, but it was to no avail.

There wasn't any life in his eyes. His thirst for murder was insatiable. He killed with rage and impunity, and it was almost entirely against women. His lust for murder ignited a city-wide hysteria. The entrances to Central Park were blocked daily by frustrated New Yorkers. They wanted answers and they weren't getting them. The demonstrations grew. The chants of, "We are not afraid. You will never win. United We Stand," the demonstrators shouted as the police looked on.

The police knew they had to get into the mind of the Westside Killer. He was becoming unpredictable. He had changed his method of operation or so they thought, and this puzzled them. It was time to not only tie him to the murders but to bring him to justice.

***

Rain had taken the day off from work and traveled with her husband to the family estate. Kelly and Blair were at work when they noticed the two detectives speaking with their supervisor. She pointed in their direction. They were terrified as the detectives approached.

"Can I have a word?" one of the men said, as the supervisor led them to her office.

"Sure," they replied.

"You two are friends of Mathew Hall and Ashley Simmons?"

"Yes," they continued.

The detective doing the talking had a grim look on his face. "Your friends are dead. Murdered."

"Murdered? Oh, God! Are you serious? Do you know who did it?" a shaken Kelly asked.

"We're still investigating, but they were killed last night. Do either of you know their family's whereabouts?"

"You would have to ask her," Blair said, pointing at Kelly.

"The person who knows is not in town. I can have her call you." The detective handed her his card. He and his partner continued talking to their supervisor.

Kelly was inconsolable as Blair tried to console her. He was stunned as he held her in his arms. Minutes later, their supervisor informed them they could take the rest of the day off. When they got to Blair's apartment, Kelly called Rain.

"Hey, Kelly, how are you? I hope this isn't about Tatyana and that fool. I warned her." Kelly didn't reply. "Kelly?" Rain said in a concerned voice. She was crying.

"It's Matt, he and Ashley were murdered last night at their apartment."

"What! Oh, God, no, no!" she screamed.

Jerry was talking with a relative and heard the screams. He ran to her. Taking the phone from her; he asked, "Who is this? Hello! Hello!" Kelly was speechless. She handed the phone to Blair.

"It's me."

"Blair? What's going on?"

"It's Matthew."

"What about him?"

"He and Ashley were killed last night."

"What? Fuck! Are you fucking serious?"

"Yeah, the police came by the job."

"Okay, tell you what, we are on our way."

"We are at my place."

"We'll be there."

***

The ride back to the city was a somber one, to say the least. The two didn't talk much. Rain cried throughout the ride. Jerry tried his best to comfort her. They were astounded by the news. No sooner than they arrived, Kelly gave her the card. The two women spoke at length. Blair and Jerry couldn't make sense of it. Jerry felt terrible. He was the one who had gotten Matthew beaten up, and now that he was dead; he was filled with remorse. As they drove home that night, Rain saw the look on his face and told him that he wasn't to blame.

"I feel awful."

"Jerry, it's not your fault. What happened had nothing to do with you. Don't do this to yourself. Don't you think like that, promise me you won't."

"I promise."

EPISODE

40

Rain called the detectives early that morning. They asked her to come in. They filled her in on the details. She told them everything that she knew about the victims. The police assured her they would contact their relatives immediately. She was bereaved as she and Jerry left the precinct.

The Westside Serial Killer had changed their lives immensely. Rain wasn't so sure about remaining in the city. Jerry empathizes with her but explains to her that they need to remain in the city. She understood but was fearful like most New Yorkers.

Rain and Jerry were home with Blair and Kelly when the doorbell rang, it was Tatyana. She wasn't aware of Matthew and Ashley's death. Rain and Kelly called her numerous times but got her voicemail. They felt it was better to tell her to her face. She was surprised upon hearing the news. She was devastated.

"Who did it?"

"The police believe it was the Westside Killer," Rain said.

"The Westside Killer? They lived on the Lower Eastside. He's never killed a guy before, or did he?"

"We don't know."

"Was it random or were they targeted?" The ringing of her phone interrupted them.

"Who was that?" Rain asked.

"Jordan."

"Why did you bring him here?"

Before Tatyana could respond, Jerry said, "Tell him to come on up." Rain was upset. Soon there was a knock on the door.

"Hi, oh, wow! I didn't know everybody was here. What's the occasion?" He quickly noticed that Tatyana and the other women were crying. "What happened? What's going on?"

"Matt and Ashley are dead," Jerry said.

"What? Dead? When? How?"

"Yesterday. Matt was shot and Ashley was suffocated with some chemical, and her neck was broken."

"Damn, that's terrible. Who would do such evil?"

"The police think it's the Westside Killer."

"They need to get this guy off the street. I saw the image of him on television a few nights ago. This is terrible. I'm sorry guys. So, what's next?"

"The police are now in the process of contacting their family."

"That's good."

The group talked for some time, and they all agreed that the killer had to be caught. It was a major concern of every citizen. Rain admonished Tatyana later that night about bringing Jordan along with her. She warned her that if she continued seeing him, she was going to stop speaking to her.

***

After the family of Matthew and Ashley claimed the bodies; arrangements were made for them to be flown home. The group made reservations to attend both funerals. The family was kind enough to keep the funerals weeks apart thus preventing any conflict. It was painful for Rain and the others. Jordan also showed up, which surprised the others. He never gave any assurance as to whether he would attend.

The days following the funerals were difficult for the group, especially for Rain. She was on an emotional roller-coaster as she reminisced on the years, she and Matthew were together. She smiled as she recalled her friendship with Ashley. They were like two peas in a pod.

***

A month later

The street lights were dim. He stood at the intersection waiting for the traffic lights to change. His car was parked a few blocks away. He began walking east toward the apartment building. A small group had gathered in the middle of the block, they were arguing as he walked by. His strides were long and deliberate as he warily kept his eyes on the group. Distracted by the group, he never saw the team of police officers.

"Police!" the men yelled with their weapons drawn.

He made a run for it. He reached for his weapon and opened fire. The police returned his fire. He ran in the opposite direction only to be confronted by another team of officers. Desperate, he tried to carjack a couple who stopped at the light, unaware of the events taking place. As he approached the couple, gun in hand, the driver drove through the red light. With the police in pursuit, he raised his weapon and pulled the trigger. But he had run out of ammunition. Trapped, he surrendered.

He was handcuffed and taken to police headquarters. He refused to say anything. When asked if he had any kind of connection to the women, he snarled and replied, "What do you think?"

The officers didn't say much after that. He requested his lawyers. He looked familiar, but they couldn't say for sure who he was. After some time, his lawyers showed up. The killer with his lawyers at his side, when asked if he knew any of the women said: "Death is inevitable and there's the belief that once a person has lived a worthwhile life and is pleased with the outcome and cause that they stood for, then the eternal sleep shouldn't be something feared. It should be looked upon as my work is done. I have fought the fight. Some I have won and some I have lost. But it was a cause that I was willing to die for. There are some things in life that we all want and seek, regardless of age or amount of success.

So, what is it that is unique and is indulgent for any man to exploit? I will tell you what it is; it's satisfying that need, that rush, that urge, which is a culmination of your hard work, that's what makes you whole. And when you have achieved it, there's only one conclusion to come to, and that's; I have put in the time and now it's time to rest; time to rest the mind, body, and soul. Dreams turn into dust and blow away like the wind. Without evil, we would never recognize good. Whatever you do to me will not bring them back." He smiled. "What were you expecting me to say, huh? Oh, you thought I would give some kind of mea culpa? Is that it?" The investigators and his lawyers were stunned as they listened. He smiled.

EPILOGUE

Blair had taken a leave of absence immediately after the funeral of Matthew and Ashley. Although he and Kelly were still a couple, she hadn't been to his apartment in some time. Back from his leave of absence, he invited her, Jerry, Rain, and Tatyana over. They were surprised that Jordan hadn't shown up.

"Where is he?" Kelly asked.

"I spoke to him hours ago," Rain shared with them.

"Okay."

Blair had a tense look on his face before saying, "There's something I need to share with you guys. I hope you don't look at me any different after this," he said.

"Come on now, what could be so bad," Jerry asked.

He took a deep breath. "I'm a police officer."

"A cop? Are you serious?" Kelly asked with an incredulous look on her face. The others sat there with their mouths wide open. The expression on their faces could have stopped traffic on Fifth Avenue.

"Hold on," he said. He pulled out his cell phone and began dialing. "It's me, is it okay, now?" he said to the person on the other end of the call. Kelly, turn on the television." She did.

There were several loud gasps. They couldn't believe what they were seeing. It was Jordan. He was being led out of the police precinct in handcuffs with an army of law enforcement officers, including Blair. They were stunned.

"Now do you believe me?"

"Oh, my God," Kelly screamed.

Jerry tried to make sense of it all. "So, explain to us in detail what happened."

"I was sent by my supervisors to Le Chic after the sexual complaint's charges against Matt, which I'm quite sure you guys were aware of. Those same allegations were made against him at his prior job before coming to Le Chic. Again, let me state that Matt was the one under surveillance. It was only when Kelly and I became close, and you guys introduced me to Jordan and began inviting me to the book signings and other events did I began noticing some unusual things. I brought it to the attention of my supervisors, and I was told to keep an eye on him."

"So, what about Matt, what was the outcome on him?" Rain asked.

"It was all allegations. None of the things they said could be proven. So, we decided to move on. But I fell in love with the kindest and most beautiful woman ever. I wanted to tell her, but I just couldn't. She thought I didn't love her when I told her that I didn't want her to move in with me. My reason for that was my undercover work." Kelly pouted her lips and smiled as the others looked on.

"So, Jordan killed these women when he wasn't writing? Is that it?" Jerry asked.

"Yeah, and he's been at it for some time."

"This fucking guy was a nut case and I allowed him in my home and had him around my family. It just goes to show," Jerry added.

"There were others as well," he continued. "The guy was a psychopath, and he used his writing to deflect attention away from himself."

"So, do you know why he targeted Matt and Ashley?" Rain inquired.

"Kelly was upset at me for doing this. But remember all the talk of me visiting your father and cousin?" he said to Jerry. "And the conversations I had with Matt, Ashley, and Jordan? It was a feeling-out process. I wanted to know if they saw or heard anything and what they were thinking. I was also doing it with you guys, but you guys had solid backgrounds. Jordan never liked Matt. He wanted Ashley for himself. He thought she should have given him a chance. He confronted her twice and roughed her up a bit. But she didn't say anything about it to Matt. How do I know this? She reported it at the precinct. I was there when she showed up, luckily, she didn't see me, or my cover would have been blown. I wanted to lock his ass up for doing that to her. I wanted to tell Kelly, but I couldn't."

"Oh, my God!" Rain and Tatyana said aloud.

"My job was to investigate that mutha-fucker. I began noticing his behavior and one night I followed him, but I lost track of him. To this day, I don't think he knew that I was following him. He got to Ashley first. Several witnesses said they heard a loud noise like a door slamming, around the time he forced her inside the apartment. He waited for Matt to come home and then shot him."

They were horrified as he continued. "No wonder he would stare at us like that," Jerry recalled.

"So is Blair your real name?" Kelly wanted to know.

"Let's go so they can talk," Jerry suggested to Rain and Tatyana.

"No, no. I want you guys to stay." They remained seated. "My name is not Blair, it's Stephen Parker."

"So, when were you going to tell me all this?"

"Kelly, I couldn't tell you then. It was protocol."

"Was it protocol when you were fucking me? I bet it wasn't." They couldn't believe what they were hearing.

"Kelly, I love you. I do."

"So, what about all the things that happened in your life, are they lies too?"

"The things that I told you about my past life are true. Nothing I told you about that is a lie. I just couldn't tell you that I was a cop, and I couldn't tell you my real name either."

"I'm confused. You lied."

"I didn't lie. I was doing my job. I love you. Yes, we can move in together now that this is over. I have no intention of being with anyone else and if you say no, I will show up at Le Chic every day until you say yes. Oh, I can't do that, because I will look like a stalker." They all laughed.

"Guys, can we have some "we" time," Rain said to him and Jerry.

"Say no more. Come on, Stephen," Jerry said. They laughed, leaving the women alone.

"Kelly, he's a cop. He was undercover. He was doing his job. What about that you don't understand? You don't think I'm upset? Of course,

I am. He had us all under surveillance the whole time. You damn right, I'm upset. But the guy loves you, can't you see that?"

"Yeah, Kelly, he loves you. I think you would be a damn fool not to stay with that man. Besides, he's got a good job." The three laughed. "You are always telling me to get it together, now it's your time to get it together. You think you had it bad, look at who I was dating, a mutha-fucking serial killer. He could have killed me. So, you should be glad that at least your man is on the good side of the law. Give the guy a chance," Tatyana explained to her.

"You guys think I should give him another chance?"

"Yes," they said in unison.

"Sis, I was worried about you. I'm glad that you are okay. Didn't you notice anything unusual with him?"

"No. He would stay up late whenever I was there. His place was clean, and everything was neatly placed and put together. All he did was type and talk about his manuscripts and books. But you know what, one night I was there, and I saw a small trunk. He warned me never to touch it. I never did. The way how he said it, now when I think about it; it was kind of weird, and he warned me in a sort of mean-spirited voice."

"I'm glad that Blair, I mean Stephen was able to get his ass. Now the city can go back to being normal," Rain added.

Later that night, Jerry took them to his favorite restaurant. Although Matthew and Ashley's relationship was short-lived, the time they spent together, and their friendship will surely be missed. Yet the others knew they had to live. Kelly and Blair moved in together. Tatyana returned home. Rain and Jerry stayed in the city.

Jordan had waged war against a city that had experienced a number of deadly and horrific events in the past, and his bloody psychopathic killing spree brought back a lot of terrible memories.

One week later

Rain and Kelly were having lunch when her phone rang, it was Blair.

"Stephen?" she said, surprised. Kelly didn't know what to think.

"Yeah, I tried calling Kelly, but it went straight to voicemail. Is she with you?"

"Yeah, hold on." She handed her the phone.

"I'm sorry, babes. I forgot it was off."

"It's okay. What I'm about to tell you, I want Rain to hear." She put him on speaker. "The ballistic on the gun that Jordan used to kill Matt, matched the ones that killed your friend, Samantha . . ."

"Oh, fuck! He killed her? Oh, my fucking, God! I was living with a monster. Oh, shit, I can't believe it."

"Calm down, Kelly," Rain pleaded with her.

"It wasn't just her," Blair continued.

"What do you mean?"

"The ballistic also matches the weapon that killed, Alonzo."

"This is way too much. He did that too, huh? What the fuck!"

"I'm sorry, babes."

"Thanks for letting me know. At least, I now have some closure."

"Yes. I'll be home late tonight. Love you. Take care, Rain."

"You too, Stephen."

"I'm so sorry, Kelly," Rain said, comforting her, as they sat there in disbelief.

Life for the friends had come full circle, and sometimes choosing to live is a more painful form of death. The friends chose to live, despite the odds they faced. The path they took was one of redemption. It was about understanding their vulnerability, and while doing so, taking back the things they lost, and taking control of their lives.